Units

Mad Dogs 8

Brenda Cothern

Units
Wench Publishing, Inc.
All Rights Reserved.
Cover: © Brenda Cothern Books, Inc.
Cover Art: Brenda Cothern

ISBN-13: 978-1-943949-33-5
ISBN-10: 1-943949-33-6
First Printing December 2017

Wench Publishing, Inc.
136 E. 145th Avenue
Tampa, Florida, 33613 USA

Other Titles

Shadows
Soul Stealer (FREE)
When Beasts Bite
Barely Restrained
Embracing Sin
Shattered Illusions
Shadows (Bundle)

Guns & Hoses
Fire & Ice
Spark & Blaze
Then & Forever

Brothers by Bond

Undercover Love

Those Who Dare
The Gardeners
Training for Revenge

Stand Alone Free Reads
Cresting Tide
New Beginnings
Coming Home
Before There Was
Beer Pong

Mad Dogs
Sixth (FREE)
Deployed
Mad Dogs vol.1
Extraction
R&R
Mad Dogs vol.2
SNAFU
AWOL
Mad Dogs vol. 3
Allies

I.N.E.T (#1)
I.N.E.T. (#2)
I.N.E.T. (#3)
I.N.E.T. (#4)

The Witch's Brew

Goddess of Fate
Retrieval
Reunion
Revelations

Dedication
To all of my fans that keeping asking for more…
Without your love of the Mad Dogs, they
wouldn't continue to share their missions!

Acknowledgements

Special thanks to JT Roadhouse in Tampa for
letting me treat their bar like my personal office.

Beta team… without you the Dogs would be a
mess!
Lora, Melissa, and Shirley… thank you for all you
do to polish my stories! I love you guys!

Glossary

These characters appear in no particular order and descriptions include the current status of the Mad Dogs.

Order – is comprised of a thirteen member Council of supernatural beings whose sole goal is to ensure the human world does not discover the existence of supernaturals. To reach this goal, they utilize the Mad Dogs to counter the Organization's efforts to expose supernaturals and recruit humans to their ranks.

Organization – is comprised of an unknown number of supernatural species who believe human should be ruled over because of their inferior status. Humans are frequently targeted for slaughter or to be turned into vampires and supernaturals that cannot be swayed to their ideology are killed.

Watchers – is a natural organization that observes and gathers information on both the Order & Organization. It is overseen by the Imperial vampire Sebastian and comprised of several supernatural species.

Lieutenant Colonel Matthew "Rex" Rolex, Councilman for the Order was turned in 1918. He was pack mates with McCormick, O'Tool, & Hunter before he took the newly formed Mad Dogs representative position on the Council in 1944. Rex was assassinated during the rogue Councilmembers' attempt to take out the Mad Dogs in 2015.

Sergeant Major J. Dick "Coredick" McCormick was turned in 1926. He became the Mad Dogs Commanding Officer in 1958. Prior to this promotion, he was pack mates with Rolex & O'Tool. He was killed in 2015 during the rogue Councilmembers' attempt to take out the Mad Dogs in 2015.

Master Sergeant / MSG Xavier "Oh" O'Tool was turned in 1942. His specialty is Recon / Intel. He became the Team Leader and pack Alpha in 1958. In 1974, he bonded with El. He is pack mates with Rolex, McCormick, Higgins, Clearwater, Rodriguez, Sullivan, and Hay. He became the Commanding Officer in 2015.

Sergeant First Class / SFC Lawerence "El" Clearwater was turned in 1968. His specialty is Munitions / Demolition. In 1974, he bonded with Oh. He is pack mates with O'Tool, Higgins, Clearwater, Rodriguez, Sullivan, and Hay. In 2015, he became First Sergeant / 1SG and 2nd in Command of the Mad Dogs.

Sergeant First Class / SFC Oliver "Doc" Higgins was turned in 1984. He is the team Medic. In 1988, he bonded with H. In 2014, he was bitten by Hay and his virus mutated. He now absorbs blood through his skin which allows his virus to consume other viruses. He is currently pack mates with O'Tool, Clearwater, Rodriguez, Sullivan, Hay, Hunter, Jordy Mitchell, Nick Swanson, Gabe Bower, Paul Williams, & Doug Fuller. In 2015, he became, pack Alpha, Team Leader, Unit Alpha Team Leader and was promoted to First Sergeant / 1SG.

Sergeant First Class / SFC Hector "H" Rodriguez was turned 1984 and bonded to Doc in 1988. His specialty is Communications. He is currently pack mates with O'Tool, Higgins, Clearwater, Sullivan, Hay, Hunter, Jordy Mitchell, Nick Swanson, Gabe Bower, Paul Williams, & Doug Fuller. In 2015, he was promoted to Master Sergeant / MSG.

Sergeant First Class / SFC Markus "M" Sullivan was turned in 2009. His specialty is Sniper. During the claiming process with Hay in 2014, his virus mutated giving him the ability to shift into a third form which has not happened in over 100 years. He is bonded to B. He is currently pack mates with O'Tool, Clearwater, Rodriguez, Higgins, Hay, Hunter, Jordy Mitchell, Nick Swanson, Gabe Bower, Paul Williams, & Doug Fuller. In 2015, he became Unit Bravo Team Leader and was promoted to Master Sergeant / MSG.

Staff Sergeant / SS Brian "B" Hay was turned in 2014 and bonded to M during his turning. His specialty is Sniper. After dying later that year, he was turned by two different species of vampire into the first ever wolf-vampire hybrid. His vampire Sires are Duke Şerbănescu & Alec Koval. He is currently pack mates with O'Tool, Clearwater, Rodriguez, Higgins, Sullivan, Hunter, Jordy Mitchell, Nick Swanson, Gabe Bower, Paul Williams, & Doug Fuller. In 2015, he was promoted to Sergeant First Class / SFC.

Master Sergeant / MSG James Hunter was turned in 1910. He was pack mates with Rolex & McCormick before he went rouge in 1966 and joined the

Organization. His specialty is Recon / Intel. In 2015, he returned to the Mad Dogs and the Council verified that he had been a double agent. He is currently pack mates with Higgins, Rodriguez, Sullivan, Hay, Jordy Mitchell, Nick Swanson, Gabe Bower, Paul Williams, & Doug Fuller. During claiming with Sullivan & Hay, his Mad Dog virus mutated to give him a third form which also allows him to speak telepathically in his human form with which he completed the claiming process. In 2015, he was promoted to First Sergeant / 1SG.

Duke Şerbănescu, Imperial, turned vampire, and former Watcher whose obsession with the Mad Dogs resulted in his dismissal from the Watchers, being released by his Sire and having all knowledge of the Watchers gathered information and procedures erased from his memory in 2014. He is one of two Sires to Hay. Currently, his physiology is changing to align with that of born vampires and also linked with B based on promixity.

Jordy Mitchell, previous Shadows' employee, is a born panther shifter who was claimed by the Mad Dog pack in 2015. He is married & bonded to Nick Swanson. He is currently pack mates with Rodriguez, Higgins, Sullivan, Hunter, Hay, Nick Swanson, Gabe Bower, Paul Williams, & Doug Fuller.

Nick Swanson, previous Navy SEAL & Shadows' employee, is a born wolf shifter who joined & was claimed by the Mad Dog pack in 2015. He is married and bonded to Jordy Mitchell. He is currently pack mates with Rodriguez, Higgins, Sullivan, Hunter, Hay, Jordy Mitchell, Gabe Bower, Paul Williams, & Doug Fuller.

Paul Williams, prior Army and from Nick Swanson's original pack, is a born wolf shifter who joined & was claimed by the Mad Dog pack in 2015. . He is currently pack mates with Rodriguez, Higgins, Sullivan, Hunter, Hay, Jordy Mitchell, Gabe Bower, Nick Swanson, & Doug Fuller.

Gabe Bower, prior Army and from Nick Swanson's original pack, is a born wolf shifter who joined & was claimed by the Mad Dog pack in 2015. . He is currently pack mates with Rodriguez, Higgins, Sullivan, Hunter, Hay, Jordy Mitchell, Paul Williams, Nick Swanson, & Doug Fuller.

Doug Fuller, is a hacker and from Nick Swanson's original pack. He is a born wolf shifter who joined & was claimed by the Mad Dog pack in 2015. He is currently pack mates with Rodriguez, Higgins, Sullivan, Hunter, Hay, Jordy Mitchell, Paul Williams, Nick Swanson, & Gabe Bower. His current role in the Mad Dogs is HQ.

Hank & Bruce are retired Mad Dogs who own and operate Dad T's resort in Florida.

Rowan Knox, prior Air Force and from Nick Swanson's original pack, is a born wolf shifter. He is best friends with Chuck O'Hare.

Chuck O'Hare is a graphic designer and from Nick Swanson's original pack. He is a born wolf shifter and is best friends with Rowan Knox. His current role in the Mad Dogs is HQ.

Shanna Crystal, fae Councilwoman for the Order, believed the Mad Dogs were outdated soldiers in the war against the Organization. After abducting M & B from Camp Smokey and stealing their blood, she intended to genially engineer more hybrids like M to fight their war. To further her research, she attempted another abduction of B & M while they were on R&R. She was killed by Lawrence in the ensuing battle.

Donavan Sinclair, human mage Councilman for the Order, supported Shanna's vision of a new form of soldier to fight the war against the Organization. He was successful in creating a type of hybrid, but killed in his attempt to capture the Mad Dogs at the night club Shadows.

Julia Carmen, fae Councilwoman for the Order, became the new Mad Dogs Council Representative after Rolex's death.

Alec Koval is a born vampire (warm blooded) who became an alley to the Mad Dogs in 2014 while working together to free Nick & Doc. He also owned the night club Shadows before El burned it down during Donavan's attack.

Kira Koval is an unclassified non-human and Alec's wife.

Chamuel "Cham", fallen angel, Alec's employee.

Simon DeBlanc, illusionist, Alec's employee.

Sebastian, Imperial vampire, is the leader of the Watchers. He was Duke's Sire until he released Duke in 2014 due to Duke's inability to remain natural in his observations of the Mad Dogs.

Chapter One

The sound of the Black Hawk's rotor blades was nothing new to the men flying toward the forward operations base. The FOB was nothing new, either. The trip and their destination was par for course when a soldier.

However, Doc's mind wasn't on their travel. It was on his new team. *His* new team. He wasn't nervous about leading his first mission as Team Leader. Not having Oh or El on the mission was strange. Stranger than the additional five men crammed into the Black Hawk with them.

Four of the five born shifters who were now Mad Dogs had military experience and Doc was grateful for that. He was also relieved he would be able to communicate with four of his new Mad Dog pack mates when they were in wolf form. Unlike Hunter who could telepathically speak to any Mad Dog regardless of their form, Doc couldn't. Doc couldn't help but be slightly envious of Hunter's new ability because as Team Leader being able to talk to his team any time he needed to would only benefit them.

Thinking about logistics of communicating with the team brought his mind back to one of the soldiers among them. Rowan sat in his desert cammies and was combat ready. It was obvious this wasn't his first mission and Doc didn't doubt the man's abilities even though they had yet to execute a mission in the field together.

No, it wasn't Rowan's combat competence that had Doc catching his gaze resting on the born wolf time and time again.

Not being able to feel Rowan's emotions because he wasn't a Mad Dog was like feeling a void in the Black Hawk. Doc was bothered by this more than Rowan's lack of ability to communicate with any of the Mad Dogs when they were in wolf form.

Rowing didn't display any emotion aside from mission focus. Still, if Doc had to guess, the mission wasn't the only thing on the wolf's mind. It was clear back at Camp Smokey that Rowan wanted to become a Mad Dog. It was just as clear that he hadn't because of his best friend, Chuck. Doc had to try really hard not to resent the civilian since had the wolf not objected, Rowan would be pack right now.

Rowan's gaze shifted from his unfocused stare at the side of the Black Hawk to glance at Doc. It was as if the wolf knew Doc had been contemplating his Mad Dog status or lack thereof. Doc gave him an encouraging smile and nod before Rowan returned his focus to the unremarkable spot on the Black Hawk's cabin.

Doc forced himself to inspect the rest of his team, his pack mates. Duke, who was a Mad Dog even if he wasn't part of his pack, sat next to B and listened to the banter between B and M. H was bullshitting with Nick and Hunter while Nick's husband, Jordy, commented occasionally. Gabe and Paul mirrored Rowan's focus.

Doc wasn't surprised by the behavior any of the wolves displayed. Nick's previous pack mates would eventually learn to relax like the rest of his team. It might take some time before their ingrained standard military behavior would shift, but it would happen so Doc wasn't bothered or concerned.

What did concern Doc was that his original Mad Dog teammates seemed to be giving him space. Doc wasn't sure if it was due to his new team leader position. He doubted that was the case and they never treated Oh this way before a mission. Likely, they were still adapting to the change in leadership and giving him space to formulate their plan of attack.

Oh had been team leader and Alpha for fifty-eight years before Doc became a Mad Dog so he didn't have to experience a change in leadership. Not only leadership, but to the pack structure. Regardless of how the team seemed to instantly and smoothly adjust back at Camp Smokey, their behavior in the Hawk told Doc they hadn't finished adjusting. Doc was still adjusting as well, so he totally understood that it would take all of them time to get used to him being the team leader *and* pack Alpha.

Just the thought of being pack Alpha ignited his instinct to protect his pack mates. That in turn brought his thoughts back to the mission they were about to execute. The first mission he was to lead the team to a successful conclusion. So, Doc forced himself to think tactically where his pack and team were concerned.

He didn't have those years of experience or even the forty-two years that Oh had been working with a teammate, either. Doc only had twelve years with H and that was significantly less than Oh had with El. Doc being the team medic, who spent most of his time at a fallback position with H, only compounded his insecurity when it came to tactics. Still, he had Oh's memories. He just hoped that if the shit hit the fan he would have time to access them to find a solution.

Doc snorted at the thought. If the shit hit the fan, Doc knew there would be no time to search their combined memories for a solution. Combat didn't give time for anything aside from ensuring you or a teammate didn't end up dead. Several of the Mad Dogs glanced in his direction when he snorted. Their enhanced hearing easily picked up on the sound under the rotor blades of the Black Hawk. Doc gave them the same reassuring smile he gave Rowan before shaking his head slightly.

Everything okay? H's question was clear as day in Doc's mind.

Doc smile brightened when he met his mate's semi concerned gaze. *Yeah, all good,* Doc reassured his mate and returned his thoughts to the tactics he needed to make a decision on before they landed at the FOB.

Doc needed to decide who on his new team was going to be responsible for what once they hit the ground and headed out to meet their mission objectives: take out the Organization's operatives and any rogue Council members' mercenaries who were trying to abduct soldiers for their individual cause.

Duke and Hunter were the easiest to assign to a position for this op. Duke's former watcher status and Hunter's ability and experience on gathering information from when he was a double agent made them the perfect fit for recon. Doc was only tempted for a moment to keep Hunter at his side to utilize the wolf's ability to speak with anyone. Having Hunter able to issue his orders to the team seemed like the best choice to utilize the wolf's new skill, but Doc could see Hunter's recon experience as more important for this op. If Oh managed without someone with Hunter's ability then so could Doc.

Nick was a SEAL even if he hadn't been active duty for some time. That made placing him in a sniper spot an easy decision even though the team had two snipers already. However, Nick's husband, Jordy, was another matter. The panther shifter turned Mad Dog had no previous military experience. That didn't mean the large black man had no skills in a fight, but it did mean he had no skills to utilize pertaining to this op. Doc decided Jordy would stick with Nick and Nick could teach him the basics for being a sniper spotter.

Rowan, Gabe, and Paul were regular military. Doc read their records while on the first leg to get to the FOB. Rowan was Air Force, Gabe and Paul were Army. None of them had Special Forces training, which was something Doc would have to rectify once they returned to Camp Smokey.

Their lack of spec ops training didn't mean they were useless, though. It just meant that Doc had to decide which role to assign each man. Doc was still contemplating the regular military wolves when the Black Hawk finally set down at the FOB. All ten men crouch-ran to clear the blades of the Hawk. They had barely stood up before a soldier addressed them.

"Team leader," the soldier began. "The CEO is waiting for you. If you would follow me, SS Doring can show your men to a barracks that has been cleared for your use."

It didn't escape any of the team that the soldier ran his gaze over them all as he spoke. It was clear the man didn't know who was in charge of the Delta unit and wasn't about to make an assumption.

"M, with me," Doc said and gave the soldier a nod to lead the way.

M's expression didn't change at his order, but Doc felt his snipers surprise. Doc was sure that M expected him to order H to accompany him to meet with the FOB CO. At some point during his consideration of whom was going to do what on this mission, Doc also decided they had enough Mad Dogs to create two teams. The Mad Dogs had always consisted of a five-man team. Well, at least until B joined them.

Quick on that realization, came the thought of who would lead the second Mad Dog team. H would be the logical choice, experience wise, but he wasn't an option. Doc was sure that at some point in the future the teams would be sent on different missions. He and his bond mate wouldn't survive that type of separation.

Length of time as a Mad Dog would make Hunter the next logical choice to lead another team. However, the oldest Mad Dog of them all had been away from the pack for over fifty years. Doc wasn't comfortable with that fact.

So, that left M. He'd only been a Mad Dog for six years. Becoming a team leader after only six years of being a Mad Dog was not only unheard-of in the history of the Dogs, but Doc's only choice. However, making M a field team leader was a sound decision as far as Doc was concerned even if he wasn't sure how well his pack mate would receive the news once Doc informed the unit of the changes he was implementing.

H, Doc mentally called out to his mate. *Take the team to the barracks and dump your gear. Then, get some grub. M and I will meet you in the canteen.*

Roger that, H replied and Doc would have cringed at the formal military reply to an issued order if he hadn't felt H's amusement across their link.

M walked at his side and Doc was sure if they could speak telepathically that his pack mate would be asking him what the hell was going on. M would find out soon enough. For now, they had to meet with the FOB CO. The meet and greet was just a formality since the Mad Dogs wouldn't even be at the FOB for twenty-four hours. Their stay would only consist of a hot meal and a few hours' sleep before they headed out.

Their mission objective focused around this FOB, but the Mad Dogs wouldn't be based out of here. No, they would set up out in the miserable Afghan mountains to observe the patrols that the Organization or Council was targeting.

Markus wasn't sure what was going on. He had no idea why Doc had included him in the SITREP meeting with the FOB CO. Because of this, he had trepidations over whatever Doc's plan for him was going to be. He felt his bond mate sending calm to him while he listened to the CO and Doc discuss the current situation with the patrols. B only asked him once if he was okay and he replied affirmative.

B slid a tray of food his way once he took a seat on the bench next to his mate. H did the same for Doc. All of the team were finished eating and didn't speak until he and Doc was finished as well. Neither he nor Doc wasted any time shoveling the shitty grub down their gullets.

"Let's head to the barracks they gave us and I'll update you," Doc informed after he pushed his now empty tray away.

The Mad Dogs stood as one, as the unit they were, and fell in line behind Doc and H who now walked at his mate's side. The emotions across the pack link covered the gambit. Excitement to be on a mission again, pure focus for the same reason, curiosity, and concern and trepidation rounded them all out.

Markus had no problem deciphering which emotion came from which of his pack mates. The only emotions that were undeterminable were Duke's and Rowan's. Markus was used to feeling an emotional void in their overall numbers because of Duke. However, it felt almost uncomfortable to feel a second void when his mind unconsciously counted ten men on the team. Markus had no time to dwell on that feeling once they entered their temporary barracks.

"Alright," Doc started. "We all know our mission objectives so I'm not going to beat that horse again." Doc grinned and after receiving smiles in return, he continued, "Since there are eleven of us now, I'm breaking us into two teams."

"What?" H asked with surprise and stared incredulously at his bond mate.

"The Mad Dogs have always been five-man teams until B joined us," Doc began to explain his decision. "We work better in small units and are easier to manage. It's also easier to utilize our specialties."

"Work better?" H echoed.

"Easier to manage?" M asked and realized why Doc had taken him to his meeting with the FOB CO.

"Utilize our specialties?" B said at the same time as H and M when they spoke.

The born shifters turned Mad Dogs said nothing and Doc wasn't surprised by their silence. He was grateful for it, though.

"The Council has ordered us to recruit," Doc reminded his original pack mates. "We've already started that process by bringing in Nick and his husband along with his five former pack mates. Including Duke," Doc nodded and smiled at the vampire. "And with Hunter, that brings the Mad Dogs to twelve. Twelve is two feasible units of six," Doc explained the obvious.

"Eleven," Rowan countered. "I'm not a Mad Dog."

"Yet," H said at the same time Duke said, "Technically neither am I, but I am pleased to be considered one and an honorary pack member."

Doc sighed. "Mad Dog or not, we have twelve who are now committed to our war. Eleven of us are in the field. Eleven, which means we have enough field operatives to form two units."

"So, what the hell does that mean?" M asked with no heat in his tone.

"What that means is that we will have two field units: Alpha and Bravo," Doc answered.

"You already said that," M stared hard at Doc. "But what does that *mean*?"

"It means not only will I be the field CO for the Dogs and your Alpha, but I will also be the unit Alpha Team Leader."

There wasn't a single wolf in the barracks that couldn't feel the weight of Doc's emotions in the words he spoke just from the tone of his voice.

"And unit Bravo?" B asked because someone had to even if he already had an idea of what Doc's reply would be.

Doc met every man's eyes before he spoke, "M will be unit Bravo's Team Leader." Doc held up a hand toward his previous teammates who all looked as if they would speak at the same time. "Here is the breakdown for this mission: unit Alpha will consist of me, still as the medic even though I'll be the unit Team Leader, H on comms, Nick as my sniper. Jordy, you are going to learn how to become Nick's spotter. Once we get back to Camp Smokey, you'll learn demo from El."

"Oh shit," H snickered and ignored his mate's warning glare.

"Paul, you're going to do recon for my unit," Doc finished.

"Yes, Sir," Paul acknowledged Doc's assignment order.

"Knock that shit off, Paul." Doc grinned. "You know we don't stand on that formal shit and you don't do it at Smokey, so you sure as hell better not revert to it while we're in the field." Doc felt Paul relax somewhat as he watched a small smile spread Paul's lips.

"I don't know shit about recon, though," Paul informed.

"Don't worry about it. I have a plan for that," Doc reassured his new pack mate and Mad Dog. "Unit Bravo. M, you will be team leader and still the team's sniper along with B. Duke... Well, you'll do what you always do."

Duke smiled and gave Doc a nod. "Of course."

"Hunter, you're on Intel and recon. You have the experience and I'm sure you can handle the job." Doc met Hunter's pale eyes.

"Gabe, you're going to be Bravo's demo man. Once we get back to Smokey, you'll join Jordy and learn from El."

"Oh God," H breathed out. "Are you sure that's a good idea, Doc?"

"I'll get to blow shit up? So, fucking cool!" Gabe chortled at the same time as H.

Doc ignored his mate's question. He met the light blue eyes of his only teammate that wasn't a Mad Dog. "Rowan, you're going to have the most vital position on Bravo team. You are going to be the team's comm man and medic."

Rowan's wide-eyed expression told Doc everything he needed to know about the man's surprise even if he couldn't feel the wolf's emotions. Doc had given much thought to his decision to task Rowan as Bravo's medic and comm man. Both positions were usually held at a fallback location. Both were vital to a unit, as well. It was a gamble on Doc's part to assign both responsibilities to one man, let alone a wolf who wasn't even a Mad Dog pack mate.

Doc's only reassurance for his decision where Rowan was concerned was that Bravo had the extra man, extra vampire, Duke. It also didn't hurt that giving Rowan so much responsibility for his current unit would more than likely encourage him to become a Mad Dog sooner. Straight or not, Rowan wanted to be a Mad Dog. Doc didn't give Rowan this responsibility to ensure he joined the pack, but he was sure it would influence and nudge him in that direction.

"So, what about this mission?" M stared at Doc and raised a questioning brow. "Are you splitting us up?"

Doc couldn't help but smile and feel pleased about M's questions. They seemed to reassure him that M would be a good team leader. It wasn't like this was the first time M had led a team. He'd done the same while he was still with Marine Force Recon, but it was gratifying to see him fall back into the role after six years with the Mad Dogs.

"No," Doc answered M before he looked at the rest of the wolves. "We have too many Mad Dogs who aren't trained in their new specialties." Doc caught Rowan tense at his words, but ignored the born wolf.

"Rowan, you will shadow H to start learning comms. Paul, you'll do the same with Hunter and Duke to learn the basics for recon and Intel. M, B, Nick, get Jordy up to speed."

"Who does that leave on the ground?" Paul asked.

"All of you, but Rowan," Doc answered and felt surprise from the born shifters through their link.

"So, I'm relegated behind the lines because I'm not part of your pack?" Rowan's tone was full of anger. "I'm a soldier and can fight just like they can." Rowan nodded in the direction of his fellow born shifters.

"The fact that you aren't a Mad Dog has nothing to do with my decision," Doc replied calmly in the face of Rowan's growing anger. "In fact, putting you on comms makes up for that and even gives you the advantage of being able to communicate with all of us," Doc gently pointed out. "Being unit Bravo's medic on top of that is a gamble on my part. However, it's one I am willing to take because whether you ever become a Mad

Dog or not, I feel you are the right man for the job in Bravo."

Doc's gray eyed gaze never left Rowan's light brown eyes that almost looked amber in the muted light of the barracks. Doc still couldn't feel the wolf's emotions through the pack link, but that didn't stop him from reading them based on the man's body language. Rowan appeared relieved that he wasn't assigned the fallback location because he wasn't a part of the Mad Dog pack. He even appeared slightly embarrassed that he had suggested such a thing.

"Rack out," Doc ordered and it still felt weird that he was the one saying the words instead of hearing Oh issue them.

All of the men moved to follow his order. That was one more thing Doc was adjusting to because aside from his teammates following his orders when he cared for them medically, seeing them obey the mundane just felt weird. He was sure he'd get used to it, used to being the Mad Dogs Team Leader and Alpha. Shit, field CO now that he'd split the team into two units.

Doc gave himself a mental shake. Now was not the time to be thinking about the changes to the Dogs that they all would need to adjust to and accept because they had no other choice.

"Rowan, with me," Doc said and didn't bother to look over his shoulder at the wolf before he walked out of the barracks.

Doc had no doubt Rowan would follow him, if for no other reason than Doc was his superior officer. He hated that was the case, but only time with the Mad Dogs would change Rowan's demeanor when one of them called him away from the team. Eventually, Rowan would feel the emotions, if or when he became a Mad Dog, of the one calling him away and usually that emotion was arousal or lust. If it was H pulling the wolf away from the group then those emotions were a guarantee.

Thoughts of his mate's desire to suck or fuck any chance he got caused a spike of arousal to course through him. He quickly stamped it out, but apparently not quick enough before his mate noticed.

You need me? H whispered in Doc's mind. *I need you and your cock in my throat.*

Not now, H, Doc replied and ignored the way his cock twitched at the thought of being buried deep in his mate's throat and totally encased by its tight hot heat.

Doc felt disappointment across the pack link before H replied, *I'll be here when you get back. As much as I want your cock to kiss my tonsils, the new pup needs you more.*

He's not a pup, yet, Doc corrected his mate.

Yet, H echoed and said no more before Doc stopped next to a stack of surplus supplies some distance from the barracks they'd been assigned.

Chapter Two

Doc stopped and leaned against the pallet of supplies. Rowan followed him out of the barracks closely enough that he didn't even have the opportunity to watch the wolf approach. Still, Doc didn't need that opportunity to observe the wolf to see the trepidation that caressed the man's body like a lover before a rough fuck.

The somewhat reassurance in Rowan's body language Doc had witnessed after he clarified why he designated Rowan to the position of comms and medic for Bravo was gone. In its place was the return of anger, shame, and insecurity regarding his value to the pack Doc had witnessed at Camp Smokey. Doc needed to fix that shit and he had every intention to fix it now.

"You're a member of this team whether you're a Mad Dog or not," Doc started with conviction in his tone once Rowan stopped before him. "You are here. Fighting a war you knew nothing about a week ago and that makes you part of this unit." Doc met Rowan's eyes with the stare of conviction. "Duke isn't a Mad Dog and not pack, but he is still part of this team." Doc paused and gave Rowan a chance to speak. The born wolf took it.

"He's a life drinker," Rowan pointed out as if that made a damn bit of difference. His next words obviously proved Duke's species made every bit of difference. "He can't become a Mad Dog. He can't join a pack. Whether he fights this war alongside of the Mad Dogs doesn't change those facts."

"No, it doesn't, but he is still a valuable member of this unit," Doc defended Duke's place on the team.

"But he's not a Mad Dog," Rowan countered.

"He is in spirit," Doc corrected. "Is that what is eating you up? You don't feel like you add value to the team if you are just a Mad Dog in spirit?"

Rowan grunted and looked away. Doc was sure he had hit a nerve. Hit the root of the problem. Rowan *wanted* to be a Mad Dog. He wanted to become part of the pack even if it meant accepting the shift in his sexuality. The fact that Rowan would go from straight to gay didn't even seem to bother the wolf at all. That actually surprised Doc since most straight men, or wolves, didn't accept lightly a shift in their inbred sexual orientation.

Doc was tempted to speak again to prompt Rowan to answer, but he forced himself to remain quiet. Several long silent minutes stretched out to the point where Doc thought Rowan wouldn't reply at all.

"I want to be a Mad Dog," Rowan started. "Just the thought of being able to talk to another in wolf form is incredible. Knowing I can do what I love and be able to talk to my brothers-in-arms if we fight an enemy in wolf form is mind blowing."

Doc waited for Rowan to continue, but the man fell silent again. He was sure Rowan had more to say. He was just as sure as the silence stretched that he would have to prompt the man.

"So, the only thing holding you back is Chuck," Doc didn't ask, but stated with certainty.

Rowan's head shot up and his light brown eyes locked on Doc. Doc knew Rowan's best friend was the only obstacle stopping the wolf from joining the Mad Dogs pack. Rowan didn't say anything while they stared at one another, but the born wolf didn't need to say a word. Doc might not be able to sense Rowan's emotions, but he could clearly see the anguish in the wolf's gaze. Rowan wanted one thing, but the man that owned his heart wanted something else entirely.

"Does he know how you feel about him?" Doc asked softly.

"No," Rowan answered after swallowing and clearing his throat. The one-word response to Doc's question sounded like gravel to Doc's ears.

Doc maintained Rowan's gaze which was a mix of confusion, hurt, and desperation for a solution to his problem concerning Chuck. Doc never expected his team leader status to include his current interaction with a teammate. Oh had never had to deal with this type of shit, so Doc didn't even bother to search the Mad Dogs' memories for the best way to handle the current situation with Rowan. Instead, he just went with his gut.

"So, you don't know if he feels the same?" Doc asked as neutrally as he could manage.

Rowan snorted. The sound was full of self-disgust and made Doc's gut tighten. "Chuck is *straight*, so it doesn't matter how I feel toward him," Rowan spat out as if reminding himself of his best friend's sexual orientation hurt to the point that anger was the result.

"Okay." Doc nodded. "I'm gonna play devil's advocate here and likely piss you off. Which, by the way is totally okay." Doc grinned. "If Chuck is straight and you think you don't have a chance in hell with him...

Because that's what you think, right?... Then why does it matter so much doing something you want so badly?" Doc raised a questioning brow at Rowan.

"He's my best friend," Rowan answered. "We've known each other since we were pups. Hell, he shifted into his human form three months before I did, but never left my side."

Doc hid his confusion at the information Rowan had just shared. Nick had told them that they were born shifters and Jordy and Nick's previous pack mates were proof enough. However, Rowan's words made it sound like born shifters were born and stayed in their animal form until puberty.

The thought made Doc realize how little he actually knew about born shifters. If they, shit he, was going to bring born shifters into their war against the Organization then he needed to know everything about their potential allies whether they became Mad Dogs, pack, or teammates. He needed to talk to Nick and pick the born shifter's brain to learn as much as he could, aside from what he'd already learned of their genetic makeup. Doc pushed the sudden thoughts about what he didn't know about born shifters away and refocused on his team member.

"You feel obligated to him," Doc offered even though he didn't believe that was the case.

"Obligated to what? He's my best fucking friend and I don't want to lose that!" Rowan's tone was defensive.

"A best friend wouldn't want you to do something that would make you unhappy." Doc almost cringed at his words. He wasn't a psychologist, but his reply sounded like something a counselor would say.

Rowan just stared at him and Doc prayed the man would say something. Anything, because the longer the silence spread out between them, the more Doc felt like a shitty team leader. A team leader should be able to guide his teammates and Doc was sure as shit convinced he wasn't guiding Rowan at all.

"You're right," Rowan finally stated softly before he unexpectedly moved.

Doc was caught off guard by Rowan suddenly closing the distance between them. His surprise at his teammate's sudden appearance in his personal space was not so great that he stepped back or responded defensively. Anyone else may have thought Rowan was attacking, but Doc wasn't anyone. Doc had six inches in height and a good thirty pounds of muscle over Rowan, so even if his teammate intended to attack him Doc knew how that would turn out.

That wasn't to say Doc wasn't attacked when Rowan connected with his body. Doc instantly wrapped an arm around the man's waist. He gave no thought to restraining Rowan's hands and didn't stop the man from pawing at his desert cammies. Doc also gave no thought to opening his mouth to enjoy the practically violent kiss Rowan assailed on his lips.

Deep down, the new team leader Doc knew he was, thought he should discourage Rowan from his current molestation. Especially since Doc was more than aware Rowan was straight. Still, the feel of the born wolf pushing against him from chest to knees and pushing him into the side of the surplus crates stacked on a pallet next to them was too much for Doc to resist.

Rowan's hands were fisting in Doc's sandy blond hair and Doc couldn't stop the moan that escaped his throat. He also couldn't resist flipping their position. One step and spin smoothly spun them until Rowan's back was against the pallet. The change in their position didn't stop Doc from returning Rowan's hungry kiss. What did stop him was Rowan's hand shifting from his hair and hesitantly pausing at his waist.

Rowan was just as hard as he, but the man's hesitation was like a splash of ice-cold water to Doc that reminded him the man he pressed against was straight. Doc pulled out of their heated kiss and rested his chin on the top of Rowan's head.

"This isn't something you should do impulsively or in the spur of the moment," Doc informed him and tried to ignore the unexpected hard-on a straight guy had pressed against his thigh.

"I want to be a Mad Dog. I want to be part of the pack," Rowan whispered softly against Doc's chest.

"I know." Doc rubbed his hands up and down Rowan's ribs in an effort to comfort the man. Comfort him how or from what, Doc had no idea.

They remained pressed against one another for several minutes and Doc really didn't want to break the moment by speaking or moving away.

"I don't want him to hate me," Rowan finally whispered to break the silence. "I won't survive, couldn't live, if he did."

Doc rubbed his hands over Rowan's back and held him. He wasn't sure what to say and knew he sure as Hell wasn't qualified to give advice in this situation. He wanted Rowan to become part of the Mad Dogs' unit and part of his pack, but he wouldn't take advantage of the wolf's suddenly impulsive decision.

"Then you need to talk to him," Doc whispered over the top of Rowan's head. "Either tell him how you feel about him or how badly you want to be a Mad Dog and join our pack."

Doc held Rowan's hips in place so the wolf had no choice but to stay put when Doc took a step back. When Rowan lifted his head and met Doc's gaze, Doc's heart broke just a bit. The want and indecision that shone from Rowan's light brown eyes was so heartbreaking his mate reached out to him.

What's wrong? I'm on my way. H asked and informed in the single mental message.

No, I'm fine, Doc told his mate. *Don't come out. I'll be there soon.*

"I'd bring you into the pack right this minute, but I think you need more time to sort out what you want and where you are with Chuck." Rowan leaned forward and his head fell onto Doc's chest. "The Mad Dogs, which you are a part of, and the pack will be here," Doc assured.

"I'm part of the unit, but not a Mad Dog or pack."

Rowan's reply was full of sadness and made Doc's heart ache worse. He continued to rub his hands up and down Rowan's arms as the man hugged his waist.

"We will still be here," Doc whispered.

Rowan only hummed to acknowledge he had heard Doc. His arms never loosened their grasp around Doc's waist and Doc was content to hold the wolf again and offer whatever comfort he could until they eventually had to return to their temporary barracks.

O'fuck thirty came way too early for all of the Mad Dogs. It had nothing to do with being awake before the sun was even up and everything to do with their lack of sleep before they reached the FOB. Doc was aware that he and Rowan were less rested than the rest of the unit, but that didn't stop him from being the first one up and ready to go.

Doc still felt trepidation over their first mission he was to lead, but he wasn't so nervous or doubtful that they wouldn't do anything less than meet their objectives. As the pack roused, Doc forced himself into a tactical mindset. He observed the team as they bantered while they geared up. Doc was grateful his mate, M, B, Duke, and Hunter seemed to be at ease about their mission. Their demeanor encouraged the born shifters to relax, as well.

Before they started to head out, Doc checked in with Oh at HQ. HQ being Camp Smokey. He was sure if Oh could feel his relief from their contact, his old team leader would have. Instead, Oh, then eventually the civilian Doug, gave him an update on where they were supposed to go once they left the FOB. Doc had a vague idea of where he was taking the team before he checked in with Oh, but hearing his old team leader confirm where he thought to take the unit was reassuring.

Doc handed over the comms to H and let his mate finish getting their Intel from their newest civilian Mad Dog. Once H finished, he plugged in the coordinates into the GPS on his wrist. A touch of a button sent the information to the rest of the unit.

Doc pressed the mic at his throat, to not only test their comm devices, but also to ensure that everyone received the info before they moved out. The coordinates they received were just a general location. Doc would decide if that would become their field camp once he had gotten a look at the area.

"Let's move out." Doc nodded to the wolves. None of them replied, but just fell in step behind him and H.

They all felt the eyes of the soldiers stationed at the FOB following them as they moved out. Enlisted and Commissioned soldiers always watched Special Forces team members. Some with curiosity, some with envy, but all of them with respect. The Mad Dogs ignored the stares following their progress out of the FOB. The newest Mad Dogs did as well, and Doc was pleased they were following the lead of their new teammates.

It wasn't until they were roughly a quarter of a click from the FOB that M spoke. "Doc." He waited for his teammate to look over his shoulder. "Do we need a marching order?"

They weren't walking single file toward the rocky outcrop of the mountains in front of them, but they weren't spread out specifically either. Doc understood what M was actually asking. Oh had always led them from the front even though he was team leader. Doc and H had always marched in the middle of the pack since as the medic and comms men, they were the most vital to the unit's mission success. If an enemy took out communications or medical, it would be a huge blow to the team.

Subconsciously, Doc fell into the position Oh always occupied on a mission. However, until Rowan was trained, it was a poor tactical position for Doc and H to be the wolves leading the unit up the mountain.

"Duke, Hunter, Paul," Doc began without looking at the men he addressed. "Take the lead. Duke, scout ahead. Hunter and Paul, one-meter spread from Duke. Hunter start training Paul."

There was no need for Doc to add 'quietly' to his order to Hunter. They all knew to speak softly to prevent their chatter from bouncing off the mountainous rocks around them.

"Ten meters out,"

Doc gave Hunter and Paul the distance he wanted them from the team. The men nodded and Doc didn't move the rest of the unit until he was confident the three men were far enough ahead to fulfill his order.

"B, you, Gabe, and Nick take point." Doc waited until the wolves were three meters ahead of him before he turned to M. "You, Nick, and Jordy bring up the rear. Start his spotter training." M gave him a nod. "You're with H and me," Doc said to Rowan and started to move out.

Rowan didn't display any emotion when he nodded his confirmation of Doc's order. Still, Doc wanted to think the man was relieved and felt reassured by his positioning with Doc and H. After giving his orders to the rest of the unit, which didn't feel as weird or uncomfortable as Doc thought it should, he was sure Rowan understood his marching order position meant his education on his new specialties was about to begin.

Doc, Rowan, and H walked abreast with roughly a meter between them before Doc sent his mate an order mentally. *Start training him on comms.*

On it, Doc could hear the seriousness in his mate's tone. He also sensed his mate's pleasure and determination to execute the order.

Satisfied the unit knew what they needed to do, Doc resumed scanning the rocky terrain. All the wolves in the unit would be doing the same regardless of Doc's order to start Nick's original pack mates training. Situational awareness was ingrained in every soldier. Even more so in every wolf.

The intricacies of the communication equipment in the comm center at HQ wasn't difficult to learn after Oh showed him the basics. In fact, Doug had to stop himself from drooling over all of the military tech that was now at his fingertips. He was sure that if he could feel Chuck's emotions, the wolf would be just as excited. Chuck may only be a graphic designer, but he was one hundred percent positive anyone who knew anything about computers would be excited by all of this tech.

"Now you know how to communicate with the team in the field."

The sound of the Mad Dog CO's voice pulled Doug's thoughts away from the tech and Chuck before they could stray even further into Chuck's behavior toward Rowan.

"How often will they require support from HQ," Doug asked and looked up from the keyboard he was itching to use.

"They shouldn't, but since the Council has decided to cut out the regular military as a middleman for check-in's and monitoring, you'll have plenty to do." Oh held Doug's hazel-eyed gaze.

Oh couldn't decide if he liked the fact that the unit was now self-sufficient. It wasn't like the Mad Dogs relied on the regular military for much, but having them monitor the team's progress while the pack was deployed was all Oh had ever known.

The unit's new civilian Mad Dog seemed more than confident when it came to all the equipment that would be utilized to support the team. Not only confident, but excited and determined to do whatever he could to help the Dog's mission be successful. Hell, Oh could even admit that the wolf displayed a confidence with using the tech even he didn't have.

If Oh hadn't been able to access McCormick's memories of how all the shit worked, they would have been screwed. That thought made him inwardly groan. He could feel his mate's amusement across their link and shot El a glare.

"Do you know how to access our memories?" Oh asked the civilian.

"H and Doc taught us before they left," Doug answered.

Oh nodded. "Mine are in there as well."

"But we're not pack," Doug interrupted with a confused frowned.

"It doesn't matter…"

"But how…" Doug interrupted again.

Whatever patience Oh miraculously possessed so far to train the wolf, popped like a soap bubble. "If you'd shut the hell up," Oh growled. "I'll fucking explain."

Oh. El sent across the link he shared with his mate. He was surprised his lover's temper hadn't made an appearance sooner.

Doug only blinked at the CO's sudden flare of anger. He saw from the corner of his eye Chuck take a step back, but Doug never took his gaze away from the now pissed off CO. Instead, he kept his trap shut and waited for the wolf to continue.

Oh took a deep breath in an attempt to calm himself. He also reminded himself that the wolf who currently occupied the seat where H usually sat was not only new to the unit and pack, but also a civilian.

"Accessing the memories of any Mad Dog, past or present, is possible. It takes more work and practice to access those who aren't directly your pack mates," Oh began. "To access mine, or any Mad Dog who is not a direct pack mate is done by going through a direct pack mate."

Doug grinned. What his new CO explained sounded just like piggybacking on a user's account when they logged on to get into the mainframe. He immediately started sifting through H's memories that were communications related. Most were field related, but there were a few that showed him H's activities in the comm room. From there, he shifted his concentration to his CO's memories of the comm center. There weren't many, and Doug wasn't surprised since the wolf had been the team leader for so long.

"What you're going to want to do..."

"Got it," Doug interrupted and ignored Oh's glare. "You don't have many of being in here. So, who am I looking for that you were pack mates with who knows this stuff?"

Oh didn't even have time to be pissed off over being interrupted again before he was surprised the wolf beside him had already accessed his memories through one of his previous pack mates.

"McCormick," Oh answered and ignored the twinge of heart ache that made itself known in his chest. "Coredick," Oh added so the wolf would know McCormick's nickname as well.

Doug nodded. "Anything else I should know at the moment?"

"No," Oh replied because he was still thrown off balance by how easily the wolf had picked up on how to surf their memories so fast.

"Then I have some catching up to do." Doug smiled. It would be like watching user manuals instead of reading them. He couldn't wait to get started.

"Sir," Doug added.

Oh growled before he just nodded and headed for the door with El following behind him.

Chapter Three

Chuck would've been standing out of the way in a corner if the communication center had defined corners. It didn't. The room looked like something straight out of a sci-fi movie or maybe just NASA's mission control. It was a hexagon and there were large screens on three of the walls across from the door. Two rows of computers and other tech that Chuck didn't recognize were laid out to match the floor plan in front of the screens.

Currently, two of the three screens were displaying a Delta unit logo. The middle screen showed a satellite image of Afghanistan. The image from space wasn't zoomed in enough to even see the details of cities. In fact, if Afghanistan had not been displayed in the upper left-hand corner of the screen, Chuck was sure he'd have no idea where in the world he was looking at.

His attention stayed on the screen while Doug spoke to Doc then H. He continued to stare at the satellite image even when Doug started talking to the other wolf. The CO of the Mad Dogs. The Mad Dogs that his best friend wanted to join.

Just thinking of Rowan made his gut clench and his heart hurt. They had had their disagreements and arguments in the past, but never like what they'd had before Rowan deployed with this unit of werewolf soldiers.

This wasn't the first time Rowan had deployed and left Chuck behind to worry about him. Rowan had been doing it for years since he joined the Air Force. Chuck just couldn't seem to get used to their separation nor would he ever become accustomed to the worry and fear over Rowan's safety. However, this time was a thousand times worse than any he'd experienced in the past. Rowan had never deployed without reassuring him that he'd return. He sure as hell had never deployed while angry with Chuck. Just knowing his best friend refused to speak with him before he deployed scared the shit out of Chuck.

Rowan didn't need to be distracted by their disagreement when he should be focused on staying alive and coming home to Chuck. Rowan's distraction, his anger, was Chuck's fault and Chuck knew it.

The gut-wrenching jealousy he felt when Rowan stated he wanted to join the Mad Dogs, regardless if it changed his sexual orientation from straight to gay, caught Chuck off guard. Not only off guard, but sparked anger at the thought Rowan was actually willing to become gay for a bunch of wolves he didn't even know in order to fight a war in which he didn't even need to risk his life.

His anger had nothing to do with homosexuality. No, it had everything to do with his jealousy that Rowan would become gay for other people. Other people and not Chuck. His feelings were beyond rational, especially since he hadn't even realized he was *in* love with his best friend as opposed to just loving the wolf as a brother.

The realization was a shock and actually came too late. It explained his feelings, but he hadn't realized he was in love with his best friend until Doug's words sank in after they watched the Mad Dogs deploy.

Rowan doesn't hate you, Chuck. He'd never hate you because he loves you too much for that.

Chuck understood Doug was referring to how much Rowan loved him as a friend. However, the last two nights while sleep evaded him, Chuck replayed Rowan's drunken behavior and the words he thought his best friend mumbled before he passed out.

I'll take what I can have.

Chuck hadn't given any thought about how he and Rowan were anything other than best friends, which were closer than brothers, before last night. Now that he looked at his irrational jealous behavior and anger at the thought that Rowan was willing to have sex with men to become part of the Mad Dogs pack which would effectively make him gay, along with the drunken words Rowan mumbled, Chuck couldn't help but wonder if his best friend felt more than just friendship toward him.

If that was the case, then Rowan's distraction level on his current mission would be even higher. The thought made Chuck's heart beat faster from fear that Rowan could be so distracted he could end up injured. Or worse, dead.

"You okay?" Doug asked after he swiveled his chair around to face Chuck.

His old pack mate had been standing against the wall next to one of the large flat screens mounted in front of them. When the CO raised his voice, Chuck stepped back even further until he was plastered against the wall. Doug thought nothing of it until after Oh and El left and the silence in the comm room was only broken by Chuck's suddenly harsh panting.

Chuck flinched out of his thoughts about Rowan when Doug spoke. "What?"

"Are you okay?" Doug repeated, and didn't hide the concern in his voice.

The comm center wasn't brightly lit, but Doug had no problem seeing Chuck with his enhanced wolf vision. The guy didn't look good. In fact, he looked on the verge of panic, but for the life of Doug he had no idea why. Nothing that had happened since they entered HQ nor anything the CO said should've caused Chuck to panic. Doug briefly thought about standing and going to his previous pack mate to offer comfort. He didn't, though. Instead, he waited for Chuck to answer.

"I'm not sure," Chuck admitted and wasn't ashamed.

Doug was only slightly taken aback by Chuck's reply. He wanted to ask questions for clarification of what was causing Chuck to have a 'freak out' moment. However, he was pretty sure the cause had something to do with Rowan and how the two wolves left things when Rowan deployed with the unit. So, he didn't ask a damn thing. Now was not the time. Later would have to be the time.

Right now, Doug had too many Mad Dog files to sift through in their memories so he could operate all of the tech that surrounded him and give the pack the best support he could so they could complete their mission safely.

"Okay." Doug gave Chuck a smile.

If Chuck really was freaking out over something Rowan related, then getting the wolf involved in the unit's comms might be just what Chuck needed to ease his nerves.

"Come over here." Doug spun a swivel chair and patted the seat.

Chuck stepped over and eyed up the chair. He had no idea what Doug was planning, but he took the seat just the same.

"Okay, now what?" Chuck asked Doug when Doug didn't immediately speak.

"I've got some research to do in their memories," Doug began and ignored the wrinkles that appeared between Chuck's eyebrows which indicated the wolf wanted to frown. "So, why don't you monitor the unit's movements."

"All right," Chuck agreed and turned toward the workstation. "Tell me what to do."

He needed to be told, too, since even though he recognized the keyboard and joystick, he had no idea what to do with them. The screen above both displayed the satellite picture of Afghanistan, but he still had no idea what he was supposed to do in order to track the Mad Dog's movements.

"Just a sec," Doug deferred.

Chuck watched as Doug's eyes seemed to slightly glaze over. He knew the wolf was searching the Mad Dogs' memories to find the information they needed. For a moment, Chuck felt envious of Doug's new ability. He refused to let himself dwell on the feeling and instead waited for his old pack mate to get back with him.

"Okay," Doug finally said and leaned toward Chuck. "Here's what you need to do."

Doug typed in a few codes on the keyboard and Chuck memorized every move, every key pressed, so he'd be able to do it on his own in the future. A red dot appeared on the satellite picture of Afghanistan after every time Doug hit enter. The dots looked small on the map, but Chuck easily counted eleven.

"All right, that's the unit. I put them all in and when we do this," Doug pushed a button on the joystick and moved it forward. "We can see their heat signatures fully."

The more Doug zoomed in on the Mad Dogs, the more each wolf's distinct outline became on the Afghanistan satellite image. Chuck stared at the wolves who now glowed bright red on the screen in front of him and the wall above the consoles where they sat.

"We should also be able to see any other heat signatures that might show up near them," Doug informed.

"Who is who?" Chuck asked because not only did he want, shit need, to know which one of the humanoid red shapes was Rowan, but he felt it was information he should know in case something bad happened.

"Here," Doug tapped a few more buttons and names appeared near the unit members.

"So, now what?" Chuck looked back at Doug expectantly. "We just watch?"

"Yeah." Doug nodded. "You watch while I do my homework which should help us help them if the shit hits the fan."

Another spike of fear for Rowan's safety clawed at Chuck's stomach. He'd never felt this level of fear when Rowan had deployed before, but then again, he'd never been immersed in his best friend's missions, either.

"And if we see something? How do we let them know?" Chuck's eyes never left the image that was labeled as Rowan, which walked between Doc and H.

"Here." Doug handed Chuck a headset equipped with a mic. "This key here will allow you to contact H. He's the com man. So, if you see something, like other heat signatures, you just want to press this to give him the heads up."

"Okay. Got it." Chuck put on the headset and gave Doug a nod.

"Good. I'm glad you're here to help." Doug gave Chuck a genuine smile because he really was glad Chuck seemed to be coming around at least enough to help him monitor the Mad Dogs on this mission. "I'm going to do my homework, but here if you need something."

"Okay." Chuck returned his attention to the monitor in front of him.

"Oh." Doug grinned. "If you want to listen in on them, just hit this key."

Chuck gave him a nod and Doug hoped his decision to let the wolf listen in on the unit's communications amongst themselves wasn't a mistake. The last thing he or the unit needed was Chuck freaking out when the shit started going down.

Hell, Doug could admit to himself that he wasn't even sure how he'd react once the killing started. Because there *would* be killing, of that he had no doubt. However, he'd deal with whatever his reaction would be when the time came. He only hoped he wouldn't have to deal with Chuck's reaction too much when they got to that point of the unit mission.

Chuck focused on the eleven heat signatures shaped like bodies on the screen before him. He moved his mouse cursor over Rowan's name and hit the key Doug told him would allow him to hear the team. He didn't hear anything. He tried again and still his headphones remained silent. With a frown he replayed what Doug had told him about listening in on the team.

A sigh of relief left him when he realized the equipment wasn't malfunctioning and he would only hear the team when they queued up to speak with one another. So, until he heard one of the Mad Dogs' voices in his ear, Chuck forced himself to pay attention to all of the red bodies that moved across the satellite image instead of just the three who walked abreast in the center of his screen.

They were halfway up the mountain when Doc, H, and Rowan caught up with Hunter and Paul. Duke was nowhere to be seen, but Doc didn't even give that fact a second thought. The vampire could be standing invisibly next to his pack mates or off scouting further along the mountain. It only took a few minutes before M, Nick, and Jordy caught up so they were all regrouped at the coords Oh had had Doug give them as a potential field base.

The Mad Dogs took positions covering every direction ensuring Doc, H, and Rowan was covered. Everyone was crouched down and Doc was grateful they had shed their desert cammies for ones that blended almost seamlessly with the surrounding mountainous terrain. The fact they had to do so after they arrived at the FOB pissed Doc off regardless if they had brought the change of clothes for a 'just in case' precaution.

He didn't blame Oh for the incorrect Intel on what uniforms they would need even though he should. Oh usually had his Intel on point. So, he was either misinformed or just not back on track after losing McCormick and Rolex, along with being promoted to CO. So no, Doc didn't blame Oh. Doc pushed thoughts of Oh from his mind. He especially pushed those away that reminded him of how much he missed his team leader. They only reminded him that *he* was now the team leader.

Doc scanned the rocky outcrops he could see from their current position. Oh's decision to send them to these coords was evident by the several caves and many hidey-holes he could spot. Looking back the way they had come, Doc could see the FOB in the distance. Their position was well beyond the patrol route of the FOB soldiers which was exactly where Doc needed the unit to be in order to meet their mission objectives.

Somewhere in the mountains surrounding them, Organization operatives and rogue Council member mercenaries were preying on US soldiers. That predation was one Doc and the Mad Dogs had every intention of putting an end to. The unit was close, but Doc didn't take the risk of speaking too loudly to inform them of their next move. Instead, he pressed the button at his throat and spoke to his team.

"Looks like a cave at our two o'clock," Doc informed. "Can I get confirmation and specs?"

"On it," Hunter's quiet voice whispered in their ears.

Before Hunter and Paul had even moved three feet, Duke's voice whispered just as quietly to the team. "Entrance four feet wide, opens to roughly ten, ceiling around fifteen. Passageway in the rear, but unexplored yet."

"Explore that passage, Duke," Doc ordered. "We are headed your way."

Duke didn't reply and Doc really hadn't expected the vampire to do so since he wasn't military, even though he was now a part of the unit and an honorary Mad Dog. Doc stood from his crouched position and the Mad Dogs followed his lead. He didn't need to tell the team where they were headed since they'd all heard his exchange with Hunter then Duke's recon report.

The unit arrived at the cave within thirty minutes. Hunter and Paul, along with Duke, had already cleared the location that Doc had decided would be their field base of operations. They had been hoofing it for most of the day, but the cave was in the optimal position for their needs.

Without being told, the wolves dropped their gear and started setting up camp. Hunter, Paul, and Gabe left the cave after dropping their shit. Doc knew they would be scouting the perimeter and also looking for anything that would burn so they could have a fire. They didn't need one which was good because finding wood for a fire in the rocky terrain of the Afghan mountains wasn't going to be easy.

"The passage leads back a hundred feet before it slopes deeper underground," Duke reported as he approached Doc. "Do you wish me to investigate further?"

Doc gave Duke's inquiry some thought. After their mission in the Swiss Alps to hunt down the Arimaspi, Doc was well aware of how they could be setting up camp on the doorway of a hostile entity.

"See what you can find for at least five hundred more feet," Doc ordered Duke.

The vampire stopped his advance, nodded before he turned, and disappeared from view in the dim light of the cave as if he hadn't even been there to begin with. It was something Duke just did and even though the former Watcher had been with them for months, Doc was still adjusting to witnessing that particular behavior from the vampire.

"Rowan, check us in with HQ," Doc ordered. He didn't need the ability to feel the wolf's emotions to know he had surprised the man with his order.

"Sir?" Rowan looked over at Doc as if he didn't believe his team leader's order.

Granted, since shortly after they left the FOB, H had been running Rowan through all the comm equipment he carried and utilized while the Mad Dogs were on a mission. However, that once over didn't mean he already knew what the hell he was to do, so he looked at H for help. The fucker just winked at him and shouldered off the comm equipment. H nudged the equipment toward him with his foot once it hit the ground.

"Give HQ our SITREP." Doc gave Rowan an encouraging smile before he turned to the rest of the unit to assign a watch rotation.

Rowan only shot H another hesitant glance before he pulled the comm equipment closer to where he knelt on the cave floor. He forced himself not to overthink using the new equipment before he removed the receiver and punched in the code to reach HQ so he could do as he was ordered.

Chuck sat up right in his chair the moment he heard Doc's voice in his ear. Hunter's reply, then Duke's filled his headset before everything went quiet again. He followed the team's movement on the screen in front of him while holding his breath in anticipation to hear one of them speak again. When Rowan's voice filled his ears, he was totally unprepared. His gasp of surprise was loud even to his ears that were now covered by the headphones.

"HQ, Dogs copy."

"HQ, copy Dogs," Chuck replied what he hoped was the correct response. Silence greeted him.

Rowan's mind froze and spun at the same time. The last voice he ever expected to hear confirm his contact when he checked into HQ was Chuck's. Chuck wanted nothing to do with the war the Mad Dogs fought. He wanted nothing to do with the Mad Dogs, period. They were gay soldiers and Chuck wanted nothing to do with anyone who was gay. His best friend's behavior made that more than clear.

Rowan had left Chuck standing in the doorway of the Mad Dogs barracks three days ago and was sure his best friend would've hightailed it home the moment he stepped on the Black Hawk. Apparently, he was wrong. Still, hearing Chuck in his ear didn't explain a damn thing about why the wolf was still at the Mad Dogs' base in the North Carolina Mountains.

Granted, they hadn't been on speaking terms when they parted, but Rowan didn't think their disagreement would have been enough on Chuck's part to make him stick around until he returned from this mission. Apparently, Rowan was wrong in this regard as well.

"Rowan?"

Chuck saying his name broke Rowan out of his contemplation over his best friend in the last week they had spent together.

"Here, HQ," Rowan replied. He just couldn't say Chuck's name because he still felt too much anger toward his best friend.

Chuck felt Rowan's formal reply as if it were a punch in the gut. HQ, not Chuck, was how his best friend responded. He forced himself to bury the hurt that was suddenly eating him up because now was not the time to attempt to reconcile with Rowan. Rowan was in the middle of the mission and needed to focus, so now was definitely not the time to fix the bridge he'd broken.

"Setting up field camp at these coords," Rowan informed. However, before Chuck could confirm, it dawned on him that his best friend might not even know how to determine the coords for where he was receiving the transmission from. "Do you need our coordinates?"

Rowan prayed Chuck didn't. If Chuck did, there was a high as hell chance that their position would be compromised. Rowan was almost tempted to ask Chuck to put their CO on the line so he wouldn't have to relay their coordinates to HQ over an open line.

"No, I have them," Chuck replied after he moused over Rowan's heat signature and recorded the longitude and latitude that appeared under his best friend's name.

Once more Rowan felt surprise. He already understood Chuck had to be in the comm center to have answered his call to HQ. However, even admitting that realization didn't make what it actually meant sink in until Chuck confirmed he didn't need the GPS coords for where the unit was setting up base camp.

Chuck was working with Doug to help their mission be a success. Rowan wasn't sure what that actually meant, but he prayed it meant Chuck was coming around to the idea that at least he, if not them both, could become part of this new pack. A new pack with a worthy cause and one that would give them the ability to communicate with each other while shifted.

"Roger that," Rowan replied and was about to sign off before he added, "Chuck?"

Chuck's breath hitched at hearing Rowan say his name. "Yeah?"

"It's good to hear your voice," Rowan admitted quietly. "Mad Dogs out."

Rowan signed off before Chuck had the chance to reply. Still, the lack of ability to tell Rowan the same didn't mute the relief he felt in his heart at hearing his best friend's words. They were words Chuck knew meant they would be okay once Rowan came home. They were words that made Chuck consider what exactly he wanted from his best friend once he returned and they were words that made him think anything might be possible if Rowan felt the same about him.

Chapter Four

Rowan returned the receiver to its cradle on the side of H's pack. He still couldn't believe it was Chuck's voice he'd heard when he checked in with HQ. When he pushed H's pack away and went to stand, the Mad Dogs' comm man stopped him and was looking at him.

"What? Did I do something wrong?" Rowan thought he'd checked them in with HQ correctly from what H had taught him during their trek up the mountain. The look on the wolf's face made him doubt what he thought he'd learned.

"No, you checked us in correctly," H replied and grinned at his new teammate. Rowan wasn't a Mad Dog or pack mate, but he was a teammate and H was going to treat him as such.

"So, what then?" Rowan lifted a questioning brow and hoped the nervousness he felt over the possibility he may have fucked up didn't come through in his tone.

"Chuck was on the other end," H said evenly and raised a brow to match the one Rowan leveled on him.

"Fucking wolf hearing," Rowan grumbled and looked away. "I'm still mission fit," he declared when he shot his gaze back to H. The look he leveled on the wolf now dared H to argue.

"Never doubted you weren't." H grinned and gave Rowan a wink.

H, Doc warned his mate by just saying his name mentally to let go of his current train of conversation with the wolf who wasn't part of their pack.

It's all good, Doc, H reassured his mate and team leader before he continued speaking to Rowan.

"If I had any doubt you weren't mission fit, you would know it before Doc."

Roman continued to look at H's grinning face and actually believed what the wolf said was true. He didn't think he believed the Mad Dog because he was mated to the unit's team leader or because the wolf would protect the pack above all. These were a given. No, what made him believe H was the way the wolf informed him as if he'd be disappointed in Rowan if what Rowan had said wasn't true.

"Okay," Rowan nodded and stood. Where he was going he wasn't sure. Probably just to the mouth of the cave so he could escape what he was sure was about to become an uncomfortable conversation.

H reached out and grabbed Rowan's arm to stop him from walking away. He understood; the wolf stood so Rowan could escape him and whatever he was about to say. H normally would have cracked a joke laced with sexual innuendo to break the stress filled tension he could practically feel rolling off the other wolf. However, even he knew this wasn't what Rowan needed at the moment. In fact, H's normal sexual banter would only make the wolf feel worse and more like an outsider instead of a teammate.

Rowan glanced from H's dark brown eyes to the wolf's grasp on his arm and back again. He said nothing, but knew his expression said plenty.

"If you want to talk, I'm here," H gently told Rowan with a serious tone.

"I know." Rowan pulled his arm free. He'd already turned away when H spoke softly, "We all are."

Rowan didn't look back at H, but he did nod his head to acknowledge he'd heard the Mad Dog before he walked away.

H's gaze followed Rowan as the wolf stepped out of the front of the cave. He wasn't the only one who watched Rowan kneel and pull his weapon into ready position. H wasn't the only one who felt concern over their teammate, either. The rest of the original Mad Dog pack was just as concerned if what H felt across the link was any indication.

"The passage is clear, but still continues deeper into the mountain." Duke's return and report shifted the Mad Dogs' focus.

"We'll still post someone at the tunnel entrance to cover our six," Doc informed. "H, you take the first rotation."

H nodded and stood. He left his comm equipment where it sat on the ground in the middle of the cave. He took up his post two meters out and facing the tunnel after he picked up his weapon.

Doc turned to the rest of the Mad Dogs in the cave. "M, take Jordy and find a nest. B, do the same with Nick. I want eyes on the patrols since we don't fully know their route." The wolves turned away and walked out of the cave without saying a word. "Duke, you're going to be our support wherever we need it. Until then, just," Doc waved a hand around to indicate the cave and outside. "Do what you do."

Duke grinned and followed the snipers out of the cave. Doc still wasn't sure how to utilize Duke the best way on a mission. The former Watcher would be the obvious choice to scout, and even though the vampire wasn't military, that didn't mean he wasn't skilled and a valuable asset to the unit. However, for this mission Doc wanted to assess his new pack mates.

"Hunter," Doc keyed up the mic at his throat. "Bring your team back."

"Roger," Hunter's deep voice replied. "ETA less than fifteen."

Doc wasn't surprised at the ETA Hunter reported. The experienced Mad Dog and his new pack mates wouldn't have gone too far afield from the cave Doc chose for their base of operations.

You're doing great, H told his mate without turning away from the tunnel. He didn't send his reassurance because of anything he felt across the link. He just wanted to let his mate know that he was doing a good job being their team leader.

"Thanks, love," Doc replied out loud and smiled at his mate even though H wouldn't see him.

"At your nine," Hunter informed Rowan of their approach.

The mountainous terrain around the cave provided minimal line of sight. There were plenty of large boulders that not only obscured the cave entrance, but also made approaching dangerous for them. It also made it dangerous for the team if an enemy approached and they were caught off guard.

Doc was still contemplating how to split up his remaining four teammates when they entered the cave. Rowan was currently his sentry at the cave entrance, but

Doc needed to decide who else he would post with him. Rowan's personal history with Gabe and Paul made Doc want to post one of them with him. However, that could create its own set of problems should Gabe or Paul wish to discuss Chuck with Rowan. So, placing Hunter with Rowan seemed the best tactical choice where Rowan was concerned. However, that would result in Gabe and Paul taking up a position further down the mountain.

Doc didn't doubt the born shifters abilities, but rather thought one of them should be paired with an experienced Mad Dog since they were still adjusting to their new pack abilities. It was this that ultimately was the deciding factor for Doc and what he would do about Rowan.

"Hunter and Gabe," Doc addressed his pack mates. "Take up a position down the mountainside. I trust you to find some place in either M or B's line of sight. Paul, you're getting some shut eye so you will be ready for relief."

Hunter and Gabe headed back out of the cave to follow his order while Paul grabbed his pack and moved to the side of the cave. Less than two minutes later, the wolf was stretched out, head on his pack like it was a pillow, and asleep. Doc followed his order to Paul and mirrored the man on the opposite side of the cave before he too caught some shut eye.

Something was wrong. Doug felt agitated. Fucking antsy and frustrated. He knew what he was feeling had nothing to do with the mundane monitoring of the Mad Dogs for the last four days. No, monitoring the unit with all the tech actually gave him a hard-on from hell. So much so, Doug was sure he'd never beat off so much in his life. Of course, this was just one more thing that told him something was seriously wrong.

Noticing every move Chuck made while they were in the comm center didn't help, either. Thoughts of being fucked by or fucking his old pack mate, his straight damn pack mate, continuously distracted him from the job he was supposed to be doing in order to support the unit on their current mission.

So, Doug had no doubt in his mind that something was seriously wrong with him. He also was sure that the CO and 2nd in command were the only ones who could tell him what the hell was going on with him. As soon as Chuck came in to relieve him, Doug had every intention to seek out the older Mad Dogs.

"Anything I need to be aware of?" Chuck asked when he entered the comm center.

Just the sound of Chuck's voice made Doug confusingly hard as a rock. Doug gritted his teeth so he wouldn't uncharacteristically tell Chuck exactly what he should be *aware* of even if it had nothing to do with the mission.

Chuck walked over to the work station he'd been using next to Doug. Doug's lack of immediate reply, his usual confirmation that the unit was just patrolling, made the hairs on the back of Chuck's neck stand on end. He almost didn't want to hear the current status of the unit because Doug's lack of reply couldn't mean anything good. Still, that didn't prevent him from stopping directly behind Doug's chair so he could see the wolf's monitor.

Doug felt Chuck stop behind him. He was so close. So fucking close that Doug felt the wolf's body heat and all Doug had to do was turn around and he'd have Chuck in his arms in seconds. Instead, Doug grasped the arms of his chair so tightly they creaked from his harsh grip.

"Doug, what happened?" Chuck asked fearfully and prayed whatever it was didn't involve Rowan being injured.

Chuck's light touch on his shoulder felt like a brand through his T-shirt and sent heat straight to Doug's balls. He reacted without thought when he spun his chair, stood, and wrapped his arms around Chuck. All thoughts that Chuck wasn't a pack mate any longer, or even gay, were nowhere to be found in Doug's lust filled mind as he pressed his erection forcefully against Doug's groin.

Chuck flailed when Doug slammed into him. Not only slammed into him, but started grinding against him and kissing his neck. Doug knew he wasn't interested in him that way and Chuck was sure he had never given any indication he wanted Doug that way either.

Chuck tried to push Doug off of him, but his old pack mate's embrace was too encasing. Growl-like moans escaped Doug's throat. Just before Chuck felt Doug's hand move to unbutton his jeans, Chuck thought he heard Doug say he was sorry. He was pretty sure Doug was, too, since whatever the hell was driving Doug's current behavior it seemed the wolf was unable to control himself.

He stopped fighting Doug's groping and focused on the red button that was at the work station. It was the button that Doug had told him to use if something happened to the unit because it would call the CO to the comm center. Well, nothing was happening with the Mad Dogs in the field, but something sure as hell was happening with the Mad Dog here.

Doug was trying to get into his pants and Chuck forced himself to ignore Doug's hands and slowly turned them until his ass was practically sitting on his work station. He reached out and slammed his palm down on the red button before he went back to trying to prevent Doug from getting to his dick. Chuck wasn't very successful and prayed the CO or 2nd in command would get to the comm center before Doug got much further. He didn't think his old pack mate would rape him, but he really didn't want to find out.

"SITREP," Oh bellowed before he cursed, "Shit."

Chuck was relieved to see the two Mad Dogs hurrying toward him and Doug because Doug had managed to push his jeans slightly down his hips.

"I don't know what's wrong with him!" Chuck shouted almost fearfully as the 2nd in command wrapped his arms around Doug.

"Fuck," Oh cursed again and stood next to the civilian and one of the newest Mad Dogs in Doc's pack.

"I have him," El assured his mate.

Chuck still had no idea what the hell was wrong with Doug or what the fuck was going on. The attractive black man who was 2nd in command didn't attempt to pull Doug off him as Chuck hoped he would. No, all he did was wrap an arm around Doug's waist and put his other hand on Doug's hip to pull Doug's ass back into him. Doug was still kissing on his neck and moaning obscenely. However, when Doug lifted his head to kiss Chuck on the mouth, the CO grabbed Doug's chin.

Oh turned the Mad Dog's chin toward him and kissed Doug harshly. Doug practically melted between Chuck and El, but his hands reached out to touch Oh. That was exactly what Oh had counted on.

"You should leave," El told Chuck over Doug's shoulder as he maneuvered Doug to face his mate.

"What's wrong with him?" Chuck asked with genuine concern. He *was* concerned, too, even as he slid along the work space to put some distance between himself and the three Mad Dogs.

"You should leave," El repeated and started unbuttoning Doug's jeans.

Chuck was aware his eyes were wide. How could they not be at seeing the 2nd in command undoing Doug's jeans while Doug devoured the CO with his mouth and hands? Seeing the Mad Dog finally free Doug from the confines of his jeans made Chuck realize his were still undone and pushed somewhat down his hips. He quickly rectified that and only glanced back at the trio once before he fled the comm center.

He's gone, El informed his mate across their link.

Oh sighed with relief into Doug's mouth. The last thing he wanted was to traumatize the civilian more than he'd already been by the Mad Dog's need for blood or sex. Sex in this case. They should have realized something like this would happen when Doc brought the born shifters into the pack and left one behind. They hadn't and Oh was beating himself up at what he understood was a situation that never would have occurred under McCormick's command.

Not the time.

El's gentle rebuke came at the same time Doug moaned again into their frantic kiss. His mate's words and the sound that escaped the young Mad Dog pulled Oh's attention back to where it should be. This Mad Dog needed sex to quell his beast, but Oh wasn't about to let a full claiming with the wolf happen between the three of them. Still, that didn't mean they couldn't give Doug what he needed.

We're not claiming him, Oh told his mate across their link.

No, El agreed.

El was pushing Doug's jeans down over his hip and was grateful his mate was doing the same on Doug's other hip. El didn't release his hold on Doug's hip until he felt his mate's hand snake under his. He kept his arm wrapped around Doug's chest while he freed himself from his jeans. El had no need to stroke his cock to get hard. Just being close enough to the younger wolf to smell his scentless pheromones was enough to make his dick throb. El gave Oh a look and slight nod. They didn't need to exchange words, physically or mentally, to communicate the choreography for how they would take care of Doc's pack mate.

Oh maneuvered them until his ass was leaning against the desktop of the work station while El moved his arm from Doug's chest. El used that hand to push Doug's shoulders down at the same time he pulled the pup's hips back. They didn't have lube and there sure as shit wasn't anytime to retrieve some. So, El made use of what he had: spit. Spit wasn't the best lube, that was for sure, but it was better than nothing if not by much. However, as bad as the pup's beast needed sex, since blood wasn't an option, he doubted the wolf would even notice. So, El bent his knees, put his cock in position, and pressed forward.

Oh was still kissing the young Mad Dog when his mate entered the wolf. His back, instead of his ass, was now pressed against the edge of the work surface. Oh gave the uncomfortable position no thought since between Doug's tongue in his mouth, his fingers pinching his nipples, and feeling his mate's pleasure from being buried in the pup, the work station digging into his back was the furthest thing from his mind.

The taste of clove and ginger on his tongue registered at the same time the incredible sensation of being full. Doug's mind still felt like he was in a fog and not his at all. However, his body knew what it wanted. Not only wanted, but apparently *needed* and had a mind of its own.

Doug pushed back harshly to meet the thrust that filled him. The sensation gave him a measure of relief from a hunger he didn't yet understand. So, he did it again. And again. At some point, the taste of ginger and clove lessened and he realized he was no longer kissing the man in front of him. The man who'd dropped to his knees and now had his calloused hand wrapped snuggly around Doug's throbbing cock. The ache in his dick pulsed in time with the beat of his heart in his ears and the continuous spark of pleasure that flooded him from his prostate being nailed repeatedly.

He braced himself by grasping the kneeling man's shoulders. Stars flashed behind Doug's closed eyelids and each explosion brought another wave of relief to the ache that consumed his body. The sound of skin slapping skin and his moans were the only sounds that filled his ears aside from the sound of his beating heart. Doug didn't care as he approached his much needed climax. His body briefly tensing didn't even register before he exploded with a long, loud, and drawn out moan.

El was skilled at holding back his release until his mate came, so when the pup's ass constricted around his cock, he was able to pound through the sensation. However, the moment he felt the wolf's aftershocks start to vibrate under the palms of his hands, he pulled out. A few strokes were all it took him to cum all over Doug's T-shirt covered back.

The leather scent of his mate's release had Oh cumming all over the floor between Doc's pack mate's spread feet. Oh ignored the young Mad Dog's cum covering his fist and splashed his chest. It wasn't the first time he'd experienced either or both at the same time. Instead, he just tensed his shoulders to help the wolf who surely would be crumpled to the floor if not for he and El keeping him upright.

Doug wasn't sure how long he panted against the man's neck that he was currently using to steady himself. However long he stayed in this position, ass in the air and feeling hands on his hips, wasn't his biggest concern. No, not even who the men were, either, because he was pretty sure they could only be the two older Mad Dogs on base. Doug's biggest concern was Chuck. He remembered resisting the urge to jump the wolf's bones. He also remembered failing and pressing against his straight former pack mate as if having sex with the wolf was the only thing he could do.

"Oh God," Doug whispered, but knew the wolves he was bracketed between would hear him.

"It's okay, pup," El told Doug and stepped back, but not before he placed a hand on the wolf's shoulder to encourage him to stand.

Doug closed his eyes and allowed himself to be pulled upright. He didn't think he could look at the Mad Dogs who were effectively his commanding officers even if he wasn't officially military. He still didn't open his eyes when he felt hands at his waist tucking his finally non-aching prick back into his jeans. Movement in front of Doug made him tense.

"Open your eyes, Mad Dog," Oh ordered in a tone he knew would cause any wolf to follow his order. He may not be the pack Alpha any more, but he was *still* an alpha.

Doug did as he was told and tried not to flinch or groan in embarrassment at the realization it was the unit's CO who had been on his knees in front of him. That could only mean that the cock that had been buried in his ass belonged to the 2nd in command. He wished their roles were reversed although even that thought didn't lessen his embarrassment.

Oh ignored the way the civilian Mad Dog refused to meet his gaze. It was clear the wolf was embarrassed and even ashamed by what had just transpired to fulfill the needs of his beast. However, Doug likely wasn't even aware that what had just happened was normal behavior for a Mad Dog. None of them, Doc or the rest of his old pack, had the chance to educate the born wolves before Councilwoman Carmon deployed the unit. The deployment of the Dogs before a new pack mate, or pack mates in this instance, was fully educated was too reminiscent of when B joined the unit.

El, take him and explain things, Oh mentally ordered his mate. *Doc needs to know to expect this from his new pack mates, so I'll be here.*

El didn't reply to his mate, but instead addressed their civilian Mad Dog. "This is normal Mad Dog behavior, Doug." El put his hand on Doug's shoulder and ignored the way the wolf tensed under his palm. "Let's go and I'll finish telling you what you can expect now that you're a Dog and your education was cut short when the unit deployed."

Doug looked over his shoulder. This was the most he'd ever heard the wolf speak all combined since he arrived in North Carolina.

"Alright," Doug agreed because the last thing he wanted or needed was to be blindsided by shit like he'd just experienced.

Chapter Five

Oh only waited until El escorted Doug from the comm center before he wiped his cum covered hand on his jeans and picked up the headset from Doug's work station. Once it was comfortably settled on his head, he called his Mad Dog unit.

"Mad Dogs, HQ, copy," Oh waited for a response. He didn't have to wait long which was always a good sign.

"Mad Dogs, HQ go ahead."

The voice that responded wasn't H, but Oh didn't know any of the born wolves well enough who were now a part of Doc's pack to know which Dog answered him.

"Need the team leader on the line," Oh told the wolf and waited.

"Copy, HQ."

"HQ, go ahead," Doc's voice finally came through Oh's headset.

"Channel five," Oh replied before he changed to a channel that he and Doc would be able to talk without the possibility of the rest of the unit accidently overhearing them.

Doc had expected to hear Doug or Chuck on the line when Rowan came to get him to speak to HQ. Hearing Oh was a surprise and one he knew couldn't mean anything good for his unit. Oh telling him to change the comm channel only reinforced his feeling that whatever Oh had to notify him about wasn't something he was going to be happy to hear.

"I'm here, Oh, go ahead," Doc informed his old team leader and pack Alpha.

"Doc, you guys see any blood shed yet?"

Doc frowned. So far, aside from learning the patrol routes and watching a whole lot of nothing threatening them, the Mad Dogs had been sitting on their asses not doing a damn thing.

"All quiet here. Do you have something for us?" Doc asked and tried to keep the hopefulness out of his tone.

"Shit," Oh cursed and didn't bother un-keying the mic so Doc wouldn't hear him. "Your new Dogs are probably hungry if not on the verge of starvation."

It took a minute to absorb what Oh was telling him. Mad Dogs needed to spill blood or have sex to keep their beasts in check. New Mad Dogs tended to need one or the other more often and Doc was kicking himself for not realizing this already. Kicking himself for not having a contingency plan to ensure his pack got what they needed. He and the original pack could go for a long time before their beasts would need one or the other. They'd been Mad Dogs long enough, but B was still new enough to the unit that Doc easily remembered how he fought to control his beast's hunger.

"Fuck," Doc cursed into the receiver. "Is Doug okay?"

Doc immediately understood something had to have happened with his civilian pack mate that he left behind at Camp Smokey. If Chuck had been pack, Doug as well as Chuck would've had the outlet their wolves needed with each other. However, Chuck wasn't pack.

Hell, Chuck wasn't even gay. That thought sent a chill through Doc especially if Oh was contacting him about the new Dogs' hunger.

"Is Chuck okay?" Doc amended his question to the one he felt was the more important answer to know.

"They're both fine," Oh paused. "El and I took care of Doug."

Doc barely had time to consider that Oh and El claimed Doug before Oh continued. "He's not claimed, and we have no plans on going there, but until you and your unit are back, we are all he has."

Oh sounded resigned and Doc understood why. His old team leader and Alpha was trying to distance himself from his old pack to lessen his pain that being promoted to CO caused. Doc was empathetic enough to understand and recognize Oh's behavior. He also understood that having to manage Doug's wolf by providing sex was more mentally painful than physically inconvenient.

"Take care of your pack, Doc. Not that I need to tell you that because you are the best wolf to ensure the pack has what they need and to keep them safe."

Oh's words were sincere and Doc was sure if he were in range to sense the wolf's emotion, he would feel nothing but confidence and Doc's ability to do just that. He wasn't though, but God if he didn't wish he was.

"HQ out," Oh said before Doc could reply.

What's wrong? H asked across their link before Doc had even returned the receiver to its cradle on the side of H's comm pack.

Doc glanced toward the cave entrance. H was with Paul down the mountain acting as their first contact should any enemies approach. He had tried to shield his emotions the second Rowan gave him the receiver and Oh requested a different channel. Apparently, he didn't lock down his shields tight enough.

How is Paul doing? Doc asked instead of answering his mate's question.

Good, H replied. *Tense like he's jonesing for action, but otherwise fine.*

Doc shifted his gaze to the cave entrance where Gabe and Hunter now pulled sentry duty. Gabe remained mission focused, but the longer he stared at the new Mad Dog, the more he noticed the same signs he recognized in his mate when H's beast needed sex. It was always hard to tell when H's wolf got to that point because H was such a horn ball. Gabe was so much like H that Doc was sure that was why the almost silent thrum of need he felt from the wolf through their pack link hadn't registered.

Hunter, Doc addressed the oldest Mad Dog amongst them. He wasn't worried that his mate would overhear his conversation. *Take Gabe and feed his wolf.* Doc ignored the feeling of surprise at his order that filled the pack link from H and Hunter. *When you are done, relieve H and Paul.*

Okay, Hunter replied before Doc watched him stand and approach Gabe.

Hunter leaned down and said something to Gabe who was still kneeling. The smile that spread Gabe's lips was instantaneous and a shot of lust flooded the pack link before it was reined in. Gabe looked back into the cave and Doc met his gaze before Doc gave him a nod of permission.

"What's going on?" Rowan asked because he was more than sure something was up by the way his team leader became quiet after finishing the call with HQ. The feeling that Doc was communicating mentally only added to his suspicion that something was going on.

"Just taking care of the unit," Doc replied to Rowan and moved toward the cave entrance. "You and me are relieving Hunter and Gabe."

Rowan only glanced at the tunnel he had been facing and returned to monitor after he answered the call from HQ. He didn't ask questions about his team leader's order, but knew his backward glance would convey what he didn't say.

Doc pushed the mic at his throat. "M, how is Jordy?"

"Good," M replied honestly, but Doc felt a tendril of concern from M for why Doc was asking.

"His wolf might need to feed and I know B and Nick can cover you," Doc replied and ignored the various emotions he felt from his pack who also heard his words over their comms."

"Okay. I'll take care of it," M confirmed.

"Good. B, take care of Nick when M is finished," Doc ordered and pushed down the emotion that made him feel like a pimp again.

"Roger that," B replied.

"And what would you have me do?" Duke asked over comms.

The vampire's tone was neutral and for that Doc was grateful. He was even more grateful he didn't need to concern himself with the vampire needing anything other than blood to feed his hunger.

"You're on tunnel duty again," Doc answered as he knelt on the rocky ground near the cave entrance.

"On my way," Duke informed so they wouldn't be caught off guard by his arrival. More importantly, they wouldn't shoot his ass as if he was a hostile approaching.

"So, are you going to tell me what all this 'need to feed' shit is with my old pack mates?" Rowan asked softly as he knelt opposite the cave entrance from his team leader.

Rowan had no doubt it was a Mad Dog thing. However, for the life of him he couldn't make any sense of the orders he'd heard Doc issue. Wolves didn't need to feed like vampires needed blood to survive, so he really had no idea what his team leader had ordered the original Mad Dogs to do. Rowan wasn't a Mad Dog, but Doc and H had insured that didn't matter. They said he was still part of the unit, part of the team. If Doc didn't blow him off and instead answered his question then maybe Rowan would actually believe them.

Doc glanced over and wasn't surprised to see Rowan looking at him. He held the wolf's light brown-eyed stare and didn't look away before he answered.

"Mad Dogs need sex or blood to keep our wolves at bay. When we are deployed, a good engagement is usually enough to satisfy our wolf side. When we are back at base, sex suffices. Usually, it's not an issue when we are on a mission. New Mad Dogs need one or the other more frequently until their wolf's feel assured that they will have one or the other whenever they need it," Doc continued to explain.

Rowan knew his eyes had widened, but not to the point of shock. He was surprised to hear there was a weakness that could be exploited since his wolf's only weakness was losing his humanity if he stayed shifted for too long. Rowan couldn't help but wonder what would happen to a Mad Dog if one of their needs weren't met.

"And if they don't get what they need?" Rowan asked quietly and was almost afraid of his team leader's answer.

"We go feral," Doc answered so neutrally it made Rowan shiver.

Memories of Rowan's teachings assaulted him when Doc mentioned going feral. There were plenty of stories of shifters going feral when they stayed in their animal form for too long. Rowan couldn't imagine what level of threat that would be if the only way to prevent going feral relied on sex or drawing blood. Then again, the Mad Dogs could stay shifted for as long as they wished without the threat of going feral and sex wasn't that hard to find. So, maybe it wasn't such a bad deal after all.

However, his team leader would've already known all of this about what the Mad Dogs needed. Because of this, Rowan shouldn't have been disturbed by Doc's orders to the rest of the unit. Still, he was and knew it had everything to do with why HQ had contacted Doc.

"What happened at HQ?" Rowan couldn't stop himself from asking.

Doc just looked at him and didn't say a word. His team leader's expression wasn't one of resignation. No, it was just a steady, passive, neutral look. That was enough for Rowan to dissect what he knew about HQ. The CO and his second were still stationed at the base. Doug, who was now part of the Mad Dog pack was, as well. So was Chuck.

Everything that Doc had just shared with him seemed to nail him in the chest. Doug was a Mad Dog.

He would need sex or spilled blood which his wolf wouldn't get while being stuck at HQ. That left only sex; sex with Chuck who was his straight best friend because Rowan couldn't really see the CO or second taking care of Doug's need. Fear for Chuck outweighed any anger he should have felt toward Doug. Chuck shouldn't be put in that sort of position by anyone. If Rowan had restrained his desire for Chuck… His thought trailed off.

"Chuck," Rowan whispered softly.

"Chuck is fine. Oh and El took care of Doug," Doc informed Rowan.

Doc didn't have words for the emotions he watched flitter a crossed Rowan's face. He did have one for Rowan's expression after he informed him his best friend's status: relief. Relief, then shock.

"The CO and second took care of Doug?" Rowan couldn't believe that superior officers would do what Doc said needed to be done let alone do it for a civilian.

"He's a Mad Dog," Doc replied, but had an idea where Rowan's disbelief came from. "Rank doesn't mean the same for us as regular military. Mad Dogs always come first, even before pack links if needed," Doc explained.

Nothing else disturbed Rowan from what Doc had just told him made him feel like shit and totally worthless than Doc's explanation of Mad Dog hierarchy. He didn't need to ask where unit members, just team members, fell on the list when it came to the Mad Dogs priorities. They were at the bottom which was exactly where Rowan was since he was just a soldier attached to this unit and nothing more.

Doc didn't look away from Rowan the entire time they talked, so he saw the moment the born wolf shut down and retreated into himself. He could see the pain the wolf was in just by Rowan's body language. Doc didn't need to feel the wolf's emotions and was only slightly grateful that he couldn't. Of course, if they could feel one another, Rowan would feel how much Doc respected, admired, and supported him for his decision not to become a Mad Dog because he hadn't decided what was best for his heart yet.

Silence stretched between them and Rowan had long since looked away from Doc to scan the surrounding mountainous terrain, as he should, before Doc spoke again. "You're still part of the Mad Dog unit," he paused. "Just like Duke is."

Doc hated that he had to continuously compare the wolf to the vampire, but that was the only comparison he had for a member of his team that wasn't actually pack.

Rowan quietly grunted. There was no need to reply to his not actually being a Mad Dog. They had covered that ground already. It was ground that just thinking about made his anger spike. If it weren't for Chuck... Rowan pushed that thought aside because he didn't want to go down that confusing road again. It would get him nowhere soon.

So, instead he just settled into his position and scanned the area leading up to the cave while he forced himself not to think about how his Mad Dog teammates were ensuring the needs of their wolves were met.

Chuck holed up in his room. He had no idea what craziness had overcome Doug. He knew Doug was gay, but unlike Gabe, his former pack mate had never displayed any sexual aggressiveness. Granted, Gabe's was always light and flirty, but still had an underlying aggressiveness that clearly indicated what Gabe wanted. Doug, on the other hand, was gay, but reserved and almost shy when it came to his interaction with other men be, they gay or straight.

This was why Chuck was so confused over what had happened earlier in the comm center. At first, he was shocked and admittedly freaked out by Doug's behavior. Still in hindsight, he couldn't deny how much he actually enjoyed Doug's hands on him while Doug groped the hell out of his body.

Chuck never got hard at the time because he was too confused and slightly freaked out by Doug's sudden sexual molestation. However now lying in his bed thinking about Doug's hands on him had him almost rock hard. Chuck wasn't sure if he was hard because it was Doug, an actual man who he remembered touching him, or if it was because he thought of Rowan's hands doing the same.

More and more since Rowan was deployed, Chuck's mind roamed to the wolf more frequently than any previous time his best friend had been deployed. At first, he was sure his thoughts kept returning to Rowan because of the way they left things before Rowan followed the Mad Dogs onto the helicopter. Now, he wasn't so sure that was actually the reason, especially since he was lying in his bed with a hard-on. A hard-on that the longer he lay there, the more he was sure his stiff dick had everything to do with Rowan and nothing to do with what had transpired with Doug.

"What the hell is wrong with me?" Chuck asked his empty room.

He never looked or even thought about Rowan in a sexual way during their entire friendship; hell, their entire lives since they were pupped at practically the same time. Now, he couldn't stop the slideshow of memories of all of the times he'd seen Rowan naked, or in nothing more than briefs or a towel wrapped around his hips.

Chuck had been so lost in thought that the groan which filled the silence of his room startled him even as he realized the sound escaped his lips. That realization made him aware of his fist wrapped around his aching cock. Not only wrapped around, but almost stroking.

He didn't remember opening his jeans and pushing them and his boxer briefs down low enough to take his dick in hand. However, how his hand was currently giving him pleasure wasn't what his mind wanted to focus on. No, all he could think about was all of the times he had seen Rowan practically naked. Not only naked, but the way his best friend's muscles flexed. Rowan's arms while he shaved or brushed his teeth. His back and abs every time he put on or took off a T-shirt. The way his thighs went taut and his ass flexed when he bent over and pulled on jeans.

It was Chuck's last visual of Rowan that caused his body to tense at the same time his back arched off the bed and rope after creamy white robe of cum shot so explosively from his cock onto his stomach and chest that his hand was still practically clean while he fought to catch his breath.

"Oh God, what's wrong with me?" Chuck asked his empty room again and ignored his now soft dick that rested against his groin under the palm of his relaxed hand.

Chuck was still searching for an answer when twenty minutes later he dragged himself to the showers at the end of the hall. It wasn't until halfway through his shower when he tilted his head back to rinse his hair that another thought blindsided him.

My suddenly new feelings are going to ruin our friendship, Chuck's thought caused a chill to race down his spine and suddenly make him feel cold regardless of the hot water causing steam to swirl around him.

"He can never know," Chuck decided aloud as if the steam might spill his new feelings to Rowan.

Chuck knew himself well enough to know he wouldn't survive losing Rowan's friendship. So, the only thing he could do would be to keep these new, unexpected, and sure as hell confusing, feelings for his best friend to himself. How he'd look Rowan in the eye again, he didn't know but that was a problem for another day Chuck decided as he dried off.

He gave no thought to returning to his bedroom with only a towel wrapped around his waist. Nope, no thought at all especially since Rowan was occupying every brain cell in his head. So, he was surprised, startled even, to see Doug and the second in command standing outside his room.

Doug watched Chuck approach and wasn't surprised to see the wolf's step falter before he continued heading toward them. He wasn't surprised, either; that his old pack mate had felt the need to shower after what Doug had done to him in the comm center.

Guilt weighed Doug down as if he were buried under a hundred-pound slab of rock. El's explanation and assurance that his actions weren't his fault did nothing to make him feel better. Doug's mind was consumed by the thought of what he may have done, how far the blind lust brought on by his wolf's need, may have gone if El and his new CO hadn't arrived when they had.

The second in command looked as he had every time Chuck had seen the wolf in the past. The Mad Dog's expression was neutral, but the way his gaze seemed all too focused on him and knowing still made Chuck uncomfortable. Doug on the other hand, looked not only nervous, but devastated.

Chuck understood his former pack mate's devastation was over what had transpired earlier in the comm center. As much as Chuck wanted an explanation about what the hell happened to make Doug so sexually aggressive, he thought ignoring the incident might be the better option for them. So, he acted like nothing had happened at all.

"I'll get dressed and head down for my shift," Chuck informed the two Mad Dogs.

"Get dressed, then we need to talk," the 2nd in command said in a tone that told Chuck he had no choice in the matter.

Chuck was more surprised by how many words the second had said than the wolf's tone. He was sure this was the most the wolf had spoken directly to any of them since he arrived at Camp Smokey.

"Okay." Chuck nodded to them before he stepped into his room and closed the door behind him.

Within a matter of minutes, Chuck was dressed and facing the two Mad Dogs who were now seated on Rowan's bed across from him.

Chapter Six

Chuck was still in a daze over what he'd learned about the Mad Dogs when his ass hit his chair in the comm center. Thoughts of Rowan still occupied space in his mind as he put on his headset, as well. However, they weren't thoughts of how to ensure his best friend never found out about his new confusing feelings toward him. No, now his thoughts swirled around Rowan's desire to become a Mad Dog. Chuck understood Rowan's need and want to be a part of this new military pack and even more so, his desire to be able to communicate with one another while they were in wolf form.

Rowan had been willing to have sex with men to fulfill his desires, but Chuck couldn't help but wonder if Rowan was aware of everything he'd just learned about the Mad Dogs. If his best friend was, he never said anything to Chuck. Then again, they had spent more time not talking to one another during the week they were at Camp Smokey before Rowan was deployed than actually sharing all of their thoughts with one another like they would usually.

Chuck still feared losing Rowan's friendship if Rowan became aware of the shift in his feelings for the wolf. But, if Rowan was willing to become gay to join the Mad Dogs then…

Chuck's thought abruptly shut down when he realized the heat signatures on the large screen mounted to the wall included more than just those of the Mad Dogs and the regular military patrol unit. He leaned forward in his chair so fast that his feet which had been sitting on the chair rollers stomped down on the floor.

A few clicks on the keyboard had him calling the unit in the field. The steady beep, beep, beep in his headset that was the military version of a cell phone ring had Chuck's knee bouncing with nervous energy. He hadn't called the unit before, so he had no idea if it usually took this long for the team to answer.

Still, he never took his eyes off the heat signatures on the big screen mounted on the wall in front of him. So, he didn't miss when the Mad Dog started moving out of the positions they had steadily held for almost a week.

The beeping in his ear continued and Chuck glanced at the big red button he had hit a little more than two hours ago. He had no idea if this was the type of situation that the button was created for or not. However, as the beeping steadily sounded in his ear and the heat signatures on the screen started moving, Chuck decided he'd rather be safe than sorry. His palm slammed down on the button and he had no doubt the other Mad Dogs would be there in minutes just as they had been earlier.

M pressed the mic at his throat. "Movement above the patrol at two o'clock."

M notified the unit before he switched places with Jordy. He had been letting the panther Mad Dog get used to the sniper rifle and teaching him how to sight while he looked through the spotter scope and gave Jordy actual things to sight. He had just about been ready to instruct Jordy to sight another rare patch of foliage when the movement caught his eye.

Their switch in positions was seamless. M had made Jordy do the maneuver so many times over the last week that he was sure his new pack mate could make the transition in his sleep. Now, Jordy was pressed against his side with his leg settled snugly between M's just as it should be for a spotter.

"I count four," B informed the team. "At the same location, but moving out."

Nick was on the rifle and when he went to change their positions, B stopped him by giving him the shot rotation. He also remained keyed up so M and Jordy would hear his enemy designations as well.

"Got it," Nick confirmed without lifting his cheek away from the stock of the sniper rifle. The only movement he made was to adjust the dial on his scope to set up the shot based on the information B gave him.

"M, Nick has Alpha target," B informed his fellow sniper and mate.

"Roger," M confirmed. "We'll take Charlie."

"Roger," B replied before they went silent so the rest of the team could communicate their moves.

"Moving to flank east of the patrol," Hunter informed them.

Doc didn't bother acknowledging the older Mad Dog. Instead, he looked at Rowan who knelt several feet away from him outside the cave.

"H, Paul, flank west. Try to get in front of the patrol. I want you to get far enough in front of them to circle around. Rowan and I are going to shadow the patrol parallel."

Rowan was already standing when Doc nodded down the mountain. The wolf appeared focused, but Doc was sure Rowan felt the same as the rest of the team. While it was a good thing the patrol remained unmolested for the last week, it was actually a relief to finally be engaging an enemy. It wasn't good for the regular military soldiers, but Doc understood his Mad Dogs. They were on a mission and that meant shedding blood. It didn't matter that Doc ensured their wolves were sated within the last few hours. His hadn't been, but experience told him their wolves preferred, received greater satisfaction, from the hunt and resulting kill.

Doc and Rowan were ten meters from the cave when he heard the beeping coming from H's comm pack. Likely, Doug or Chuck was calling to inform them of the movement near the patrol, so Doc ignored the sound. He and Rowan were down the mountain half way to where H and Paul had set up their perimeter when Duke's voice whispered in their ears.

"Should I do something about this annoying noise?"

Duke's question was actually funny because the vampire had asked it so formally and seriously.

"Answer it. It's HQ. You can be our go-between," Doc ordered Duke and didn't expect the former Watcher to reply. He didn't.

"Mad Dogs field unit."

Duke's answering of the call from HQ amused every soldier on the team. He was so formal and sounded so much like a butler instead of a soldier they couldn't help but be amused. Of course, Duke leaving his mic open was the only reason they heard him in the first place.

"Why the hell are you answering comms?" Oh demanded to know when he heard Duke's polite answer to their call.

"Well, hello to you as well, Xavier." Duke smiled, picked up the comm pack, and walked to the front of the cave. He heard several snickers and chuckles in his ear, but Duke ignored the Mad Dogs' amusement.

"What can we do for you today?" Duke asked the new Mad Dogs' CO and the chuckles in his ear turned into sporadic laughter.

"Dammit, Duke. I don't have time for your shit," Oh growled into his headset and ignored the looks from Doug and Chuck who could hear both sides of the conversation. "I see your heat signature and…"

"I have a heat signature," Duke interrupted. "Hmm, that's interesting."

"Will you shut the fuck up?" Oh spat out. "Jesus Christ, why the hell did Doc leave you on comms?"

"Likely because he and the rest of the unit are creeping down the mountain and I'm the closest to this bag," Duke answered seriously and grinned. He knew Xavier well enough to know the wolf hated when his rhetorical questions were answered so Duke couldn't help fucking with the Mad Dog.

"Now is not the time, Duke," Doc reprimanded his vampire Mad Dog even though he knew Duke was enjoying hearing their old team leader on the verge of a temper tantrum.

"Roger," Duke replied to Doc before he addressed Oh. "I am acting as the go-between," Duke said seriously. "What do I need to relay to the team?"

Oh was momentarily stunned stupid by the sudden shift in Duke's behavior. It was as if a switch had been flipped and the serious, if underlying mocking tone, was now all business. Now, totally mission focused. Oh gave himself a mental shake because now was not the time to ponder how Doc had managed to make Duke a team player.

"We see fifteen hostiles closing in on the patrol," Oh informed. "Hunter and Gabe are on course to intercept five. They are forty meters out." Oh paused long enough for Duke to relay the information before he continued. "Four are west of the patrol, sixty meters out from the patrol leader. H and Paul, need to adjust course by fifteen degrees to intercept." Once again Oh paused to allow Duke to relay the Intel.

"And the others?" Duke asked.

"Moving parallel to the patrol," Oh replied and focused his gaze on the heat signatures Chuck had labeled as one through fifteen.

"Is there anything else we are required to know?" Duke inquired and waited for Oh to respond.

"Not at this time," Oh replied. "Keep the channel open and Chuck will update you on any changes you need to be aware of."

Oh could practically feel the civilians' wide-eyed stare looking at him. He didn't care. If the wolves were going to have anything to do with the Mad Dogs then Oh was going to treat them as if he would any other soldiers, any other Mad Dogs, part of Doc's pack or not. Oh removed the headset he wore and turned to face Chuck.

"You'll monitor the team," Oh ordered before he turned to Doug. "You hit your rack since you pulled the last twelve and in case they need you later."

"Is that an order?" Doug asked without breaking eye contact with the CO.

Oh hadn't expected the civilian Mad Dog to question an order and was slightly impressed the wolf did. He ignored his mate's amusement and answered, "You're not military, so no. It's a suggestion."

Doug frowned. "So, because I'm not military, I'm a Mad Dog in name only since I haven't been through boot camp," Doug stated instead of asked. "I thought the Mad Dogs were a *military* unit."

He has you there, El pointed out to his mate. *Civilian or not, we can't have it both ways. He's both a Mad Dog and military because of that or he's just a civilian who's been claimed by Doc's pack for nothing.*

Oh didn't bother to acknowledge his mate's mental comment before he answered, "you're a Mad Dog, military or not. Still, hitting your rack was a suggestion, not an order because Mad Dogs rarely *order* each other to do anything. When we do, you will have no doubt about it."

Doug relaxed at the CO's reply. He understood the wolf's reasoning. He'd been awake for the last sixteen hours and even though he'd stayed awake longer, usually while partying, feeding his beast's need made it feel as if he'd been awake much longer. However, as tired as he should feel he felt wide-awake instead.

"I'll stay and help monitor the team with Chuck for a while before I head to bed," Doug informed his CO.

Oh nodded to Doug and couldn't help but approve of the wolf's dedication to his new pack. He turned toward the door and El followed him then stopped behind him when Oh paused in the doorway.

"You both have this." Oh looked at each wolf. One a Mad Dog, the other still a wolf not attached to his former pack. Both civilians. "If one of the Dogs is injured or in threat of capture, call us."

Oh turned, ignored the expression of fear-laced concern on the civilian wolves' faces, and left the comm center with his mate following behind him.

Doug was relieved when he realized he wasn't the only one speechless after the CO and second left. Still, he refocused on the screen displaying the heat signatures. Chuck seemed just as content to focus on the Mad Dogs closing in on an enemy as he had and for that, Doug was grateful because he had no idea what to say if his former pack mate expected him to say anything at all.

Hunter and Gabe crept forward. They stayed low to the ground and at a forty-five-degree angle to the last man of the patrol that they could see. There was less than twenty feet between them and the patrol soldier, but the human was oblivious to their presence. He was just as oblivious to the enemy movement closing in on his flank behind him. Hunter didn't fault the human for his being unaware. The man wasn't slacking in his duties by any means. No, he just didn't have the added senses of a wolf to realize that he was currently prey.

He could feel Gabe's focus on their objective through the pack link they shared. Hunter could also feel Gabe's excitement to finally engage an enemy and his wolf's desire to do so. He felt the same. His wolf was just as focused and excited to take down prey even though Hunter didn't let those emotions bleed into the pack link. He was old enough, experienced enough, to control what emotions he allowed the others in the pack to feel. Gabe was just a pup, so Hunter didn't fault the new Mad Dog for his emotions that leaked into their pack link.

"Psst," Hunter hissed out so quickly the sound almost didn't register at all. In fact, it was so quiet it was barely there which was why he did it as opposed to keying up the mic at his throat to speak to his teammate.

Gabe glanced at Hunter when he heard the almost nonexistent noise. He met the older Mad Dogs amber eyes which currently looked golden from the reflecting light off the boulders surrounding them. Hunter gave a few hand signals to indicate their plan of attack. Gabe nodded to confirm he understood. He waited for Hunter to go ahead of him before he fell in behind the wolf.

H took the lead. Not because he doubted Paul's ability as a soldier, but instead because he was the smaller of the two of them. They were both shielded by the cover the boulders provided, but no matter how small Paul attempted to make his six-foot two frame, H would still be the smaller of the two even if it was only by a few inches. It was times like these that he wished he had B or M's height which didn't even reach six foot.

Still, that didn't mean he or Paul couldn't move stealthily and remain hidden behind boulders as they advanced to get in position ahead of the patrol. Paul stopped next to him so close as H looked around a large boulder to get his eyes on the front of the patrol that had H not been in the 'mission zone' he would've gotten hard from the contact.

"There…," H started to whisper the patrol's location and inform Paul they could easily skirt them to flank the enemy when the patrol leader called a halt by holding up his closed fist.

H shifted minimally so Paul could observe the patrol with him. The patrol leader had already lowered his fist and the entire patrol was squatted down close to the ground. The twelve man patrol obviously was a unit that had worked together long enough for each member to know their shit. The squatting men covered every angle and appeared ready to face any attack that may come from the mountains surrounding them.

Sadly, H knew there was nothing that could prepare the human soldiers for an attack from the nonhuman organization operatives or rogue Council members' mercenaries. The human soldiers could put up a fight, H had no doubt, but they weren't physically, shit or even mentally, capable of defeating the enemy force that was about to descend on them.

The fact the patrol leader even sensed that something could be wrong, enough to make him call a halt, was more than impressive as far as H was concerned. However, the patrol leader sensing something wasn't right didn't mean shit because sensing something didn't mean one was guaranteed to survive an encounter with the enemy.

"Doc," H pressed the mic at his throat before he whispered his mate's name.

H didn't know if he was in range of his mate to mentally communicate, but that was only one factor for why he used the unit's comms. He wanted the rest of the team to hear whatever Doc's orders were going to be before they all acted.

"I see them, H. Are you in front of them?"

"On our side," H replied to his team leader's inquiry.

"M?" Doc addressed one of his snipers.

"We see only one of the four opposite H's position."

"B?" Doc requested an update from his other sniper.

"We have two of the three that are attempting to flank the patrol's six."

"Orders?" H had asked because he and Paul could move further west to get in front of the patrol and cross over to the enemy side of the mountain. However, to accomplish that they would have to go so far ahead of the patrol if the shit hit the fan, they would be of no use to the unit at all.

"Hold your position, H," Doc ordered only moments before the shit *did* hit the fan.

The sound of gunfire bounced off the mountains surrounding the valley the soldiers patrolled. Doc cursed and moved. He felt, more than saw, Rowan on his six. The patrol was firing randomly into the mountains to their south for which Doc was extremely grateful. The last thing he wanted was for anyone in his unit to fall victim to friendly fire.

"Hunter."

The older Mad Dog's name was the only warning given before Nick took a shot. B watched through the sniper scope as Hunter and Gabe hit the ground the second Nick said the older Mad Dog's name.

B was aware they were clear of the next shot when he gave his new pack mate the information to take out their next intended target. B watched the first, then the second asshole fall to the ground. Kill shots to the chest.

"Two down," B informed over comms.

"One down," M added to B's report.

"Move in," Doc ordered. "Identify."

The patrol was firing randomly to the south into the mountains. Several of the men had been wounded and lay on the ground. Three looked dead, but Doc knew that just because the soldiers were no longer breathing didn't mean the Organization would lose interest in them. More necromancers worked for the Organization than actually were involved as freelance mercenaries.

"Delta!" Doc shouted.

"Delta!" Rowan identified himself as he and Doc descended into the middle of the patrol's flank. The humans had scattered north and south to find cover, but that didn't stop the Mad Dogs from identifying whose side they were on for this engagement.

"Delta." "Delta." "Delta." Hunter, Gabe, and Paul echoed as they closed in to cover the patrol.

H and Paul crouched down by several of the soldiers that were at the head of the patrol and had taken cover near their advancement point. The patrol leader was one of those soldiers.

"I knew something wasn't fucking right!" He spat out and ducked when a bullet ricocheted off the boulder they were crouched behind.

H didn't have line of sight to the rest of the Mad Dogs. Hell, he didn't have line of sight to shit. So, he keyed up his mic.

"M, B?"

"Another down," B informed.

"Finally got a bead on another," M added before he paused and spoke again. "Neutralized."

"Look for the others and make sure they are all fucking down," Doc ordered.

He was huddled with Rowan and two of the patrol soldiers. Doc ignored all of their looks to question what the hell he was talking about when he ordered the team to make sure they were all down. Chest shots usually ensured an enemy was down, but the Mad Dogs knew better.

"Two of four down," M's voice came over their comm's. "Duke we need info."

"Do you have more information, particularly the location of the remaining hostiles?" Duke asked HQ.

Chuck heard the vampire, but was frozen where he sat watching the red outlines of bodies moving across the screen. He was so mesmerized that he wasn't even tracking Rowan. No, he was just watching the movement of bodies and trying to ignore those who no longer moved at all, even though they still radiated enough heat for their sensors to pick up.

"Chuck!" Doug yelled and slapped him on the arm. "Answer."

Doug could've answered, but felt Chuck needed to feel like a part of the unit even though the wolf was obviously only sticking around until Rowan returned.

"They seem to be fleeing south into the mountains," Chuck finally answered the vampire. Silence greeted him for several long moments.

Duke relayed the information to the team and waited for Doc to respond. He didn't have to wait long.

"Tell HQ to monitor the direction they are headed," Doc informed Duke. "Also, let them know we will be babysitting the patrol overnight."

Duke relayed the information to Chuck and when the wolf didn't reply, figured there was nothing else HQ had to say.

"Hunter, Gabe, take care of the dead," Doc ignored the looks shot in his direction from the soldiers next to him. They were looks of disbelief.

However, he was sure their looks had everything to do with what they thought was his respect for fellow fallen soldiers; the 'leave no man behind' kind of respect. It was a respect he didn't deserve since his only reason for ordering the corpses be retrieved had nothing to do with patriotism and everything to do with ensuring the Organization or rogue forces couldn't use them to add to their army.

"H, Paul," Doc keyed up again. "Bring the wounded to base. I want everyone there."

That was Doc's last order before he stood. Rowan and the patrol soldiers followed his lead and they all followed Doc as he began the trek back to the cave.

Chapter Seven

Five of the twelve of making up the patrol were dead. It took Hunter and Gabe three trips to bring the fallen soldiers up to the cave and lay them respectfully outside of the entrance. It wasn't the first time either Mad Dog had taken care of their fallen comrades and their respect for the men who'd given their lives was evident in how they laid the men out. Four more of the patrol was injured. The Mad Dogs, Doc, Rowan, H, and Paul helped or carried them back to the cave. Doc immediately began triage and Rowan observed everything, committed everything to memory since he would eventually become a team medic.

Doc diagnosed and spat out orders that Rowan followed to a T. Rowan stuck to Doc's side as his team leader then H started treating the humans.

"Finish bandaging this," Doc met Rowan's gaze and was pleased the wolf didn't hesitate to follow his order.

Doc surveyed the cave. Only three of the soldiers in the patrol were mission fit. One of which was the patrol leader who had sensed something was wrong enough to halt his men. Doc looked at the man who was speaking in a low voice to each of his men.

Doc had no problem hearing the reassuring and encouraging words the man thought he was speaking privately. This was a soldier who sincerely cared about his comrades. Doc was still tracking the man's movements when the soldier finally stood after speaking to his last patrol mate. Doc met the man's cold blue-eyed gaze and continued holding that stare while he approached.

"Sir," the patrol leader addressed Doc. "No disrespect, but what the fuck just happened? I know our patrols have been hit before and we expect that," the soldier paused. "But what the hell? We haven't had a hard-enough time to warrant Delta shadowing us, so what gives?"

He doesn't pull his punches. Doc felt his mate's amusement just as strongly as he heard H's words in his mind.

"The frequency of attacks on patrols along this route brought us in," Doc answered seriously and with a straight face. This wasn't his first time giving a half-truth to a human in the military.

"Bullshit," the patrol leader didn't hesitate to say. "Delta doesn't get deployed to babysit patrols that *might* be hit by insurgents."

Doc held the man's stare for several moments before his gaze dropped to glance at the soldier's nameplate on the left side of his chest. "McAllister," Doc began but was immediately interrupted.

"Mac," the patrol leader corrected.

"Okay, Mac." Doc took the human by the arm and led him out of the cave.

Doc gave a nod to Hunter and Paul who had positioned themselves as sentries at the mouth of the cave when he passed. He stopped several yards away and turned to face the human soldier.

"This is above your clearance level," Doc started because he already knew the cover story he was about to tell in order to explain the Mad Dogs presence. "Insurgents have not only been attacking US patrols in the area, but taking soldiers as prisoners of war." That was the only truth Doc was willing to admit.

Mac's expression didn't change. He wasn't surprised or shocked by Doc's revelation. He wasn't pissed off over it either like Doc expected a soldier to be. So, Doc wasn't sure what to make of Mac's lack of reply.

"You're lying," Mac said with conviction because he was sure he wasn't getting the whole truth. If nothing else, Mac knew when he was being lied to. He could give his heritage credit for being able to discern whether he was being told the whole truth or not.

Doc didn't react to Mac's claim. He was too experienced from his many years of being a Mad Dog to react to someone calling him out on a lie.

"Why would I lie about our mission objective?" Doc asked neutrally and raised a questioning brow.

"I don't know. You're Delta and you bitches do black op shit all the time, so you tell me why you're giving me some 'above your clearance' bullshit answer." Mac glared at the Delta soldier who was clearly charge of this Special Forces unit.

Mac really didn't care why Delta came to his patrol's rescue when they were hit by the insurgents. He cared about his men. But it was that care for his men that made him press for answers as to why the Delta unit was even here in the first place. The fact that the Delta soldier who stood before him and every one of the men on the man's team wore no insignias didn't escape Mac's notice, either. The huge man who now stood in front of him wore fatigues, but the only reason Mac knew he was Delta was because the man and his team claimed as much when they assisted in repelling the attack on his patrol.

Sure, there was the high possibility that Delta units didn't wear patches or anything that would identify them as US military. And, the guy before him was clearly American, but what if he really wasn't working for America's best interest? The guy had already lied to him, after all.

Doc watched Mac take a step back and his hand tighten its grip on his weapon. He had no idea what could have bounced around in the man's head to make him suddenly wary. Still, having the human wig out and shoot his ass was the last thing Doc needed.

"Okay, Mac," Doc started again. "There *is* shit that is above your clearance level, but I'm not lying about soldiers being killed or abducted from patrols. We are just here to stop that shit from happening."

The Delta team leader's words rang true to Mac. However, the fact that the man didn't mention insurgents were the cause wasn't lost on him. Mac was old, had lived alongside humans for long enough, to know they and his kind weren't the only ones who occupied the world. Still, just because he was suspicious of the Delta team leader for not telling him the truth didn't mean the man was anything more than human, even if he was getting a strange vibe from the man.

"We can't call in an Evac into the cords we are at," the Delta team leader's voice broke into Mac's thoughts. "But we can call in one within a click from here."

Doc had been watching the patrol leader closely enough to where he knew his words broke the man out of whatever tornado of thoughts were starting to consume him. Doc had seen the same symptoms in other soldiers when shock started to set in, which was exactly why he spoke. He needed Mac to focus on what his men needed so he wouldn't become incapacitated by shock. Doc learned long ago that giving a soldier something to do, even if it was as mundane as checking supplies in a pack, it could stave off shock and keep them functional.

Mac studied the Delta soldier. He detected no lie in the man's words about getting his injured soldiers back to base so they could receive the medical treatment they needed. However, Mac couldn't help but believe that even though the man's words were true and actual procedure, he used them to distract him.

"What's your name?" Mac asked because he really needed to know what the large sandy-blond haired Delta team leader went by.

"Doc."

Mac looked the man over from head to toe. This wasn't the time or place to look him over sexually, but that didn't mean part of his mind didn't register the man's attractiveness. He decided he could see the Delta soldier being a unit medic, although he never thought a medic would have the position of team leader. Usually, medics and comms were fallback positions, but maybe it was different with Delta.

Doc could see the wheels of thought spinning in the patrol leader, Mac's, eyes. The soldier was analyzing everything. Everything Doc had told him as well as dissecting everything that had transpired during their engagement with the enemy. The enemies Doc couldn't even begin to guess were Organization operatives or rogue councilmember mercenaries. That was a question they might find an answer to by inspecting the fucker's who didn't survive the attack on the patrol.

H, Doc mentally called out to his mate. *Grab someone and see if we can discern who attacked the patrol.*

I'll take Hunter and Paul with, H replied, but Doc showed no sign physically that he'd ordered anyone to do anything.

Mac felt a weird disturbance in the air around him. That was the only way he could describe the creepy-crawly sensation that seemed to wrap around his body. It took everything he had not to react to the sudden and weird sensation which assaulted him. The feeling was gone almost as soon as it registered in his mind, but that didn't stop him from focusing more fully on the man before him.

Doc wasn't Fae. Unseelie like him or Seelie like the Fae that balanced out his existence. The Delta soldier wasn't a vampire, either, because Mac easily could determine the undead. Witch, wizard, or necromancer, especially necromancer, he could determine just as easily as well. The man wasn't any of these. That only left shifters.

However, in all of Mac's years, he never felt a creepy-crawly sensation when he was in close proximity of a shifter so he was hesitant to assume the man was one. What he wasn't hesitant to assume was that the man standing before him was anything as benign as just a human.

Mac's extended silence was beginning to concern Doc and make him think the patrol leader was further along in being swallowed up by shock than he originally assessed the man's mental state to be. The last thing Doc needed on top of dealing with the patrol's wounded was to have to manage their team leader if the man fell into a state of shock.

"Mac." Doc snapped his fingers in front of the man's face.

Mac slapped Doc's hand away from the front of his face. He understood Doc's gesture, but he wasn't in shock. No, he was just distracted by the shit that went down and resulted in him standing in front of a being he was sure wasn't just human. Not that he feared whatever the hell Doc was, and maybe the rest of his Delta unit were, but not knowing was distracting.

"I need to get my wounded taken care of," Mac said with a conviction he felt. He may not be human, but these humans were his and he wouldn't lose another one if he could help it.

"We do," Doc corrected and started moving back toward the cave entrance.

Mac followed Doc and moved to check on his men again while the Delta soldier knelt next to his most severely injured unit member. Mac couldn't hear what Doc was saying to Torres, but he could see his unit mate nod before he relaxed with a serene smile on his face. Mac frowned and made his way to Torres's side after Doc moved away.

"How are you doing, Torres?" Mac asked after he squatted down next to the soldier he was responsible for.

"I'm good, LT," Torres answered weakly.

"What did Doc tell you?" Mac hated that he had to ask when he should be reassuring one of his men.

"Told me I'd be fine, LT," Torres replied full of belief and confidence in the Delta medic's words even as he pushed his palm against his belly. "Told me a bird was going to get me back to base."

Mac couldn't do anything other than meet Torres' weak smile with one of his own. "That's right, Tor, we're going to get you back to base and the doc's going to fix you right up. You'll have the women flocking to you while you recover." Mac forced out a chuckle.

"My cock says the more the merrier," Torres chuckled with a pain filled grin.

"That's right, Tor. The more the merrier," Mac repeated and patted his teammate on the shoulder before he stood.

Torres' gut wound wasn't survivable. That much Mac knew from his battle experience. Even if the Evac bird was setting down outside the cave right now, Torres wouldn't survive long enough to make it to their base which didn't even have a medical unit that could handle Torres' wound. Mac knew this, but like any good team leader he reassured his soldier he'd pull through. The fact that the Delta team leader had already told his teammate the same before Mac knelt down next to Torres didn't escape Mac's notice.

Doc left the side of the patrol soldier who wouldn't live longer than the next two hours and saw from the corner of his eye Mac take his place at the man's side. There was something about patrol leader, Mac, which had Doc's warning bells ringing loud in his head. They weren't the bells he heard when there was a threat to him or the pack. No, Doc had no feeling he was being threatened when it came to Mac. But, he had some sort of feeling.

Doc was sure that if H was in range to feel his current confusion and concern over why the patrol leader made his bells ring, his mate would be asking him what was wrong. Thankfully, H was with Hunter and Paul. Doc shook off the eerie feeling he got from the patrol leader. Mac wasn't a shifter, necro, or vampire. He was just a human. A human that for some reason seemed to make Doc's hackles rise, but a human just the same.

Doc had just squatted down next to H's comm pack when M and Jordy entered the cave. He gave his pack mates a nod before he lifted the handset from the cradle. B and Nick entered the cave before Doc even had the chance to call HQ.

"Would you like me to take a sentry position while you organize the team?"

Doc glanced behind B and Nick entering the cave and met Duke's gold-rimmed red eyes. The vampire was standing a few feet from him outside the cave and Doc easily heard the sincerity in the vampire's question.

"Yeah. That would be great, Duke, thanks," Doc answered and gave the former watcher a smile before he shifted his focus back to contacting HQ.

"HQ, Mad Dogs." Doc keyed up to contact HQ. He had no doubt they had been monitoring the team's communications and locations, but Doc understood he needed to hail them directly to interact with them.

"Go ahead, Mad Dogs."

Doc didn't recognize the voice which acknowledged his call, but it didn't matter. It was either Doug or Chuck and if neither of them could fulfill his request for the Evac of the injured patrol soldiers, Doc was confident they would call Oh to the comm center.

"We need Evac for five at these cords," Doc rattled off the coordinates for where he thought was the best location for an EZ.

"Copy, Mad Dogs. Evacuation zone coordinates confirmed."

There was a pause on the line and Doc waited. There was nothing to say. All he could do was wait for HQ to give him an ETA on the bird. However, the longer the silence stretched on, the more Doc became concerned that the civilians who were monitoring his team weren't sure of what they were doing.

"HQ, ETA for Evac?" Doc finally asked.

"Sorry, Doc," the voice of either Doug or Chuck filled Doc's ear. "ETA twenty minutes."

"Twenty minutes, copy," Doc confirmed. "Anything we need to be concerned with?"

"No. All we see are you guys," the voice paused. "The others… We don't see anyone else."

"Copy that, HQ. Mad Dogs out," Doc ended the call.

He didn't allow himself time to doubt whether the Intel from HQ was accurate or not. Whether it was Doug or Chuck he'd just spoken to didn't matter. The Mad Dogs had never relied on support from HQ. McCormick always laid out their mission plan. They always knew their extraction point and backup EZ. They also knew what they had to do if they missed an extraction deadline.

Having support while they were on a mission, contacting anyone aside from a checkpoint check in, was something totally new for Doc and the pack. New or not, Doc felt a sense of relief that if he needed information or some sort of help, like the Evac, he had HQ practically at his fingertips.

Doc stood from where he was squatted next to the comm pack. He allowed his gaze to scan the men from the patrol and his pack mates.

"Evac is a half of a click away," Doc informed and pushed several buttons on his wrist GPS unit. "B, M, give us cover." The snipers were already moving before Doc had the chance to address the rest of his team.

"Jordy, Nick, and Gabe," Doc indicated his team members with a nod. "Flank. Hunter go with H and Paul. Mac you're with me and Rowan to assist getting your guys to the Evac. Duke," Doc was several feet away from the mouth of the cave, but watched Duke tilt his head to acknowledge he heard Doc. "You're with H and Paul as well." Duke nodded and moved out of everyone's line of sight from where he stood at the cave entrance.

H, Doc mentally called his mate. *You and Paul in wolf form. Duke is heading your way. Flank us.*

Roger that, H confirmed the order.

Getting the wounded into position to start their trek to the EZ took enough time for the Mad Dogs to get into position. The remaining patrol soldiers helped their brothers in arms along with Doc, Rowan and Mac. Doc only spent a moment to key up and inform his team that they were on the move.

All was going to plan and they were practically to the EZ when the attack came. The only warning they had, wasn't enough.

"Movement on our…," Gabe sent at the same time H said, *got four in front…*

"Down, down. Cover, cover," Doc shouted at the men only seconds before gunfire erupted around them.

Men and wolves scattered to find cover. There wasn't much this low in the ravine. Pain from at least two of the Mad Dogs flared through the link at the same time he heard some of the humans get hit.

"Report," Doc ordered over their comms for the benefit of Duke and the humans that were in ear shot. He also demanded the same mentally from his mate.

Can't get an accurate count, yet, H informed.

Mac answered at the same time as H, "Four more of mine are hit and two of them are taking cover across from us."

Doc nodded. *Who's been hit?* Doc asked his pack.

Not me, H reassured his mate.

"Anyone hit?" Doc keyed up.

In my thigh, Hunter informed. "*Paul's been hit. My package, in his side. Gonna need med immediately.*"

Doc's blood ran cold. There was only one reason Hunter would need medical ASAP: he and Paul had been shot with something poisonous. There wasn't much that could take them down, but who the hell knew what their enemies could have concocted that wasn't just sulfur.

"Son of a bitch," Doc cursed. *H, need you to get to Hunter and see what you can do to slow that shit down.*

I'll try. We've been separated, H informed.

Doc glanced at Mac and the two remaining injured and one obviously dead patrol soldiers that were within his line of sight. Nick and Jordy looked like they wanted to shift and tear apart whoever the hell was pinning them down, but they knew better than to do so in front of the humans.

"M, B?" Doc requested his snipers to report.

"No clear shots," M informed before B added, "Ditto."

Paul took several shots, Hunter's voice entered Doc's mind again and he could hear the pain Hunter was experiencing, even if it hadn't increased across the link. Hunter was shielding. There was no doubt.

Screaming suddenly echoed off the sides of the ravine. The humans next to Doc looked around. Their eyes were wide and Doc could practically smell their fear. However, and surprisingly, their patrol leader, Mac didn't appear to be afraid at all.

The uncomfortable sensation he'd felt earlier returned as Doc met Mac's gaze. Mac's lack of fear and that eerie feeling once again made Doc reassess his earlier conviction that the man was a human. If they survived this encounter, and Doc had no reason to think they wouldn't, he'd worry about it then.

"Duke, report," Doc requested.

B replied instead. "Five down, the rest retreating."

"We have you in sight," M added.

"Rowan, stay here while I retrieve Hunter and Paul," Doc ordered and Rowan nodded.

"I'll go with you to offer cover," Mac offered.

Doc couldn't treat Paul or Hunter with the patrol leader present even if he did suspect the man was more than just human. Mac had to stay with Rowan in case he wasn't.

"This might be what's left of your patrol," Doc started. "You're needed here."

Mac thought to argue for a moment before he gave the Delta team leader a nod. However, that didn't stop him from following the man with his eyes as he headed out to retrieve their wounded.

Chapter Eight

Doc easily followed Hunter's mental directions to his location. Neither of his pack mates was in good shape when he reached them. The soldier Hunter had been carrying lay crumpled in a pool of blood next to Hunter's seated form and it was obvious there was nothing Doc could do to help him.

Hunter had used his belt as a tourniquet around the top of his thigh and his pant leg had been cut open. The bloody knife in his hand, along with how much blood had soaked into his fatigues, told Doc that Hunter had attempted to remove the bullet.

Next to Hunter lay Paul in wolf form. Matted fur covered his flank, his tongue fell to the side of his open mouth, and he was panting rapidly.

"Did you get it out?" Doc asked Hunter as he moved to Paul.

"Maybe," Hunter replied. "Still burns in there, but Paul needs your help more right now."

Doc agreed. Hunter had slowed down whatever the hell the bullets were made of or coated with, likely sulfur, which was affecting them. So, Hunter could wait. He dropped his med kit onto the ground. It made a loud thud, but Doc ignored it as he met Paul's pain-filled gaze.

"Hunter, translate," Doc ordered since the Mad Dog was the only one who could speak telepathically with them all regardless of their form.

Paul would understand him, but Doc had no way to hear Paul unless he shifted. Shifting wasn't an option since Doc needed hands, not paws, to treat Paul.

"Going to fix you right up, Paul," Doc told his new pack mate. "Going to hurt like hell, though."

Paul whimpered. His whine only got worse when Doc assessed the wound in his side. Two holes three inches apart had hit Paul's flank.

"Exit wound on the other side?" Doc didn't want to roll Paul if he didn't have to.

"He says no," Hunter answered for Paul.

"Shit." Doc ripped open his bag and pulled several items out. "I don't know if this is sulfur or not, so I don't want to give you anything for pain before I get the shit out of you."

"I don't give a fuck. Nothing can hurt as bad as this shit. Just get it out," Hunter answered again for Paul before he addressed Doc. "What can I do to help?"

Doc didn't look at Hunter when he answered. "Keep shielding. Paul try to shield so the pack link isn't flooded with your pain." Paul managed to nod. "Hunter, lay over his shoulders."

Hunter growled in pain, but was in position atop Paul within a matter of seconds. Doc pulled out a scalpel, forceps, and hemostats. A stack of gauze pads sat by his knee.

"Hunter, tell the pack we need calm."

From the corner of his eye, Doc saw Hunter nod. His pack mates head had barely finished moving before Doc spread the fur away from the first bullet hole in Paul's flank. Three quick slices with the scalpel allowed Doc to spread the skin around the wound. He put the handle of the scalpel between his teeth before he took the forceps and hemostats in hand.

Doc dug into the wound in search of the metal that was causing his pack mate so much pain. A howl escaped Paul's throat and echoed around the ravine before Hunter clamped Paul's muzzle closed. Finding the bulk of the bullet wasn't hard and didn't take long. Doc dropped the small piece of metal on the ground next to his knee.

Now the hard part, Doc thought to himself.

Doc wiped away the copious amount of blood and searched for the fragments he knew remained. He didn't stop until he was ninety-nine percent sure he had found them all.

"One down, one to go," Doc informed. "You're doing great, Paul."

"He says fuck you, get this shit done," Hunter relayed through clenched teeth.

Doc's were clenched as well from the overwhelming pain he felt through the pack link. The thought that the rest of the pack would also be feeling Paul's pain briefly crossed Doc's mind before he repeated the procedure on Paul's second gunshot wound.

"Done," Doc exclaimed with relief and wiped away blood from Paul's still almost gushing wounds.

"No time to stitch you up pretty," Doc told Paul who's breathing was beginning to settle back to normal. "A few staples and your wolf will take care of the rest." Pain still filled the pack link, but six staples later, three on each wound, and Doc was finished treating Paul.

"Your turn." Doc met Hunter's amber-eyed gaze.

Hunter grunted in reply and moved from where he had been pinning Paul down for Doc to treat the wolf. He rested his back against the small Boulder that had propped him up before Doc arrived.

"My shields are still locked down," Hunter told Doc, in case his new team leader and pack alpha had any doubt.

Doc examined Hunter's stretched out leg. The wolf's fatigues were torn open, not cut. However, Doc couldn't say either while he looked at Hunter's thigh. His pack mate had mangled the flesh around the gunshot wound so badly that Doc couldn't even see the edges of the original hole. Of course, using a K-Bar would do that, but in reality, it only made Doc's job easier.

"You get the bullet out?" Doc asked to confirm Hunter's assessment from before.

"Doubt it, but shit is still burning more in some places than others," Hunter replied steadily as if he wasn't still bleeding and in pain. "Pretty sure those bullets were coated in sulfur."

Doc refused to look at the long scar that marred Hunter's face. They'd all become so accustomed to seeing the scar that the pack gave no thought to how Hunter became scarred in the first place or what had caused it. Sulfur was the only thing that could really hurt them and cause scars. Hollywood got their elements confused. It wasn't silver when it came to werewolves, it was sulfur. Still, Doc wasn't about to assume anything especially considering their adversaries and what Shanna and Donovan were able to accomplish before the pack took them out.

Doc nodded and got down to work. It took a lot more gauze to soak up Hunter's blood in order to find the bullet and fragments. He got them all, though. Fifteen staples later, Doc had the mess that was Hunter's thigh taking care of.

"You need to shift in order to heal this faster," Doc stated the obvious.

Hunter grunted. "And just how are you going to explain that to what's left of the patrol?" He didn't give Doc a chance to reply before he asked, "there are still some humans from the patrol, right?"

"A few," Doc answered Hunter's second question absently because his mind was still trying to find a solution to his pack mate's first question.

"But?" Hunter asked.

Doc must have let something slip in his tone or his feelings to cause Hunter to speak even though his mind was preoccupied.

"I think..." Doc looked away from his handiwork. "Mac is something," Doc paused and let his train of thought shift to the man in question. "Not necro, vamp, or shifter, but something not entirely human."

"Does Duke have any idea?"

Doc hadn't given any thought to their vampire Mad Dog. Duke used to be a Watcher and even though his memories related to anything to do with the neutral organization had been stripped from him, the vampire could likely give them an answer to what patrol leader McAllister really was.

"They haven't been in the same place at the same time." Doc decided to fix that once they regrouped. "We will see what he has to say when we get back."

H, head back to the cave, Doc ordered his mate. *Tell the others as well.*

Will do, H answered through their bond link.

Doc didn't need to tell his mate to shift back before he arrived at their field base of operations. They all knew the protocol where humans were concerned.

"Shift and I'll carry Paul," Doc told Hunter before he keyed up to relate orders to the rest of the pack. "Regroup at our last cords," Doc only paused for a moment. "Rowan, contact HQ. I want them on the line when I get there."

"Yes, sir," Rowan replied.

"You think that's a good idea?"

Doc understood Hunter was referring to him shifting and not his order to regroup. Did he think it was a good idea? No, but he needed his injured pack mates to heal as quickly as they could. That meant Hunter needed to shift. By Doc's count, there were only three humans left from the patrol. Well, two humans and whatever the hell patrol leader McAllister might be since he sure as hell wasn't human as far as Doc was concerned.

"No, but it won't matter." Doc made a tactical decision before he continued. "We need to recruit, so we'll let the chips fall where they may."

Hunter raised a brow before he began to laugh. He was still chuckling when he pushed off the ground, stood, and undressed. Within the blink of an eye and with an almost undiscernible blur, Hunter stood before him in all his wolf glory. Hunter favored his back leg, but when he stepped forward it was only with a limp.

Doc gathered up Hunter's fatigues, put them in his pack mate's back pack, and picked up Hunter's rifle. He slung both over his shoulder before he squatted back down next to Paul.

"All right, pup." Doc grinned. "Time to go."

Paul growled and Doc looked at Hunter for a translation. Doc felt Hunter's amusement under their combined pain in the pack link.

You don't want to know, Hunter informed.

Doc just chuckled and picked up Paul. He cradled the wolf against his broad chest. He also mentally informed his mate that they were heading back to the cave and that both Hunter and Paul would be in wolf form.

Mac wasn't stupid. He was more than sure the Delta team leader wanted him to stay in the cave because there was something he shouldn't see. Of course, the man thought he was a human so he really couldn't fault the team leader's precaution. There was a likely chance the Delta team leader was like him, a nonhuman, who served in the military amongst other humans. However, that likeliness only increased when the man insisted on retrieving his teammates on his own.

So, Mac tended to his remaining two patrol members. They were hurt, but their injuries were not life-threatening. As long as they weren't out here long enough for infection to set in, they would be fine.

After giving his men water, Mac focused on the Delta comm man. Rowan was his name and Mac didn't hesitate to squat down close to the soldier. He didn't 'feel' like the team leader, so Mac thought he was safe in assuming the guy was human. Mac wasn't paying attention to what Rowan was actually telling their HQ.

Instead, he was watching the entrance of the cave to be aware of when the rest of the Delta team returned.

Two soldiers walked in and immediately took up sentry posts just inside the cave entrance. Mac was too far away to see if he felt the same vibe from them as he had gotten from their team leader. A few minutes later, two more men entered. They were snipers based on the weapons he could see slung over their shoulders. Two additional Delta soldiers entered the cave fifteen minutes later.

That accounted for them all except the team leader, the two injured, and the one he'd only heard was called Duke. Mac had no idea if Duke was a call sign or the man's actual name, but he was too distracted by the Delta unit's behavior to give it much further thought.

They didn't speak to one another even though they seemed less guarded than before they headed out to the EZ. Mac didn't have a comm set like the Delta team, but he wasn't blind. If their team leader had been giving them orders, they would've replied. They weren't replying to anything and it was this strange behavior that prompted him to stand and approach the two snipers. The same feeling that he'd felt from the team leader crawled across his skin when he stopped in front of the two men.

"You really didn't have a bead on anything?" Mac asked.

"We took the shots when they came available," M replied evenly.

"You really think we'd just let... Assholes' take out the unit?" B's tone was almost angry at the insinuation he or his mate would simply allow *anyone* to bring them down if they could prevent it.

Mac met the deep green eyes of the auburn haired sniper. It didn't escape his notice that the other sniper almost said something else before he called their attackers assholes. This, of course, only reinforced his position that whoever, whatever this unit was, they were here for more than just protecting patrols.

"No, I don't," Mac answered and walked toward the mouth of the cave where the remaining Delta soldiers stood sentry.

Again, the sensation of 'more' could be felt. These men appeared just as guarded as the snipers. Still, it was almost as if they had shut down, but they were still fully aware. Mac didn't engage them in conversation, but instead just joined them in scanning the rocky terrain.

He was still standing between the Delta soldiers when their teammate came into view. The man had long black hair that was pulled back and secured at the nape of his neck. Totally not military regulation, but then again none of the Delta unit's hair were.

"You should check on your men," H said casually as Duke came closer.

Mac didn't look away from the man approaching them when the Hispanic soldier next to him spoke. He had the impression the guy didn't want him to get too close to the man approaching them.

"They're good," Mac replied. "As good as they are going to be with their injuries."

"Still…," H started at the same time Duke stopped his ascent up the ravine to reach the cave.

Caution and concern immediately filled the pack link as H and Gabe reacted to Duke staring at the patrol leader. Neither Mad Dog moved even though they felt M and B come up behind all three of them. All four Mad

Dogs heard the slight intake of breath the patrol leader took even though the soldiers hadn't moved a muscle.

"Well, this is a surprise," Duke said to himself, but had no doubt his teammates would hear him with their sensitive wolf hearing.

He had no way to inform the Mad Dogs of what they surrounded at the entrance of the cave without keying up the mic at his throat. That really wasn't an option since the Unseelie stood close enough to them all that the Fae would be sure to hear anything he said. Duke could only hope his pause would be enough to let the Mad Dogs know that something was wrong. Something that could be a minor threat. Something they currently surrounded.

Duke stood stock still until he saw H and Gabe tighten their grip on their weapons. M and B were behind and to the side of the patrol leader enough that Duke had no problem seeing them draw their 0.9 mil's. M pointed his at the Fae while B held his steady in his hand down by his thigh. Duke had no doubt B could have his weapon raised and fired in the blink of an eye if need be.

Mac watched the approaching soldier stop. He felt the two snipers step up behind him and the tension ratcheted up from the Delta soldiers surrounding him. He felt as if they were all in a standoff. Mac and the man coming up the mountain more than he and the four men who were more than human that were surrounding him. Mac still wasn't sure what the long black-haired man was, but he had no doubt the man figured out that he was Fae.

"I mean none of you harm," Mac said just loud enough that the man his gaze was focused on could hear.

Several seconds paused before Duke snorted with amusement as if the Fae could actually hurt him. In fact, there was very little the Fae could do to hurt the Mad Dogs, as well. However, that didn't mean the man was harmless.

"It may be wise to secure our new friend until Doc returns," Duke said softly, but knew the Fae would hear him just as easily as the Mad Dogs. "Do not teleport away if you have nothing to hide and do not wish to make the Mad Dogs an enemy."

The man who climbed up to the cave spoke at the same time Mac's arms were grabbed. The grip on his biceps was not painful, but firm enough to let him know that that could easily change should he resist. Mac never looked away from the dark-haired soldier even though from the corner of his eye he saw one of the Delta soldiers turn to level his weapon on him. Mac ignored him.

"Vampire," Mac finally whispered quietly so his voice wouldn't echo back into the cave and reach his wounded men's ears. There was no mistaking those red irises.

Duke smiled at the Fae. He wasn't surprised that the man recognized him for what he was since his red irises tended to give him away.

"Indeed," Duke replied and bowed his head slightly. "Fae."

"Like the councilwoman?" Gabe asked and promptly shut his trap at the glares M and B shot in his direction.

"It is more than a surprise to find one of you here," Duke continued as if Gabe hadn't spoken at all and he closed the distance between them. "Not many of you remain in this world, so I am sure you will understand our precautions."

"No, there aren't and I do not understand why you would think I am a threat to you when you are more a threat to me," Mac replied calmly.

He still had no idea what the Delta soldiers were, but he was pretty sure they were shifters. The vampire *and* the shifters were a greater danger to him than he could ever be to them. So, his only choice was to comply.

"I won't fight you as I mean you no harm," Mac assured. "But I sure as fuck would like to know what the hell is going on."

H snickered and M out right laughed. Gabe's eyes darted from one man to another and B just grinned.

"Doc can tell you when he gets back if he thinks you need to know," M finally told Mac and pulled him away from Duke, H, and Gabe.

He and B hauled Mac toward the back of the cave and far enough from the man's patrol mates so that they could talk without being overheard. Neither Mad Dog had the impression the Fae was a threat. Whether that was due to the concern and way he cared for his patrol or because of their experience with Councilwoman Carmen, they didn't know. So, they gently urged the man to sit down against the cave wall after they disarmed him.

"Do we need to restrain you?" M asked seriously.

"No," Mac replied honestly.

He had no intention of running or doing anything aggressive. He valued his life after all. Plus, his remaining men, *God, only two left*, needed him and he hadn't come across another nonhuman in almost ninety years. His men were his priority, but the Delta unit sparked his curiosity; not only his curiosity, but a desire to be around others that were nonhuman. It was a desire that caught him totally off guard and one he didn't know he wanted to feel.

"Okay." M nodded.

"I'll stay with him just the same," B informed his mate.

He really can't get out of here, M sent B through their link. B just shrugged in reply.

M smacked B on the shoulder and moved away to join Rowan. B never looked away from Mac, so he watched as the patrol leader tracked his mate's movement.

"He's not one of you," Mac said without looking at the sniper who now leaned against the cave wall next to him.

B didn't reply to Mac's reference to Rowan. Instead, he countered with, "Your men aren't like you."

Mac snorted. "If only. Most of my kind went home a long time ago."

"And you decided to stay," B commented as if he actually knew what the Fae meant when he mentioned his kind having gone home.

Mac shrugged in answer and shifted his gaze from the comm man and other sniper to the cave entrance. He wanted to ask the man next to him if he was a shifter or not. However, he didn't get the chance to work up his nerve before the vampire headed their way.

"I got this, B," Duke nodded to his child.

B met Duke's steady gaze and the smile on the vampire's lips. He couldn't speak to Duke telepathically like he could with his mate, but he didn't need to because Duke never lied. If Duke thought he was safe with the Fae patrol leader, then B had no doubt that that was the truth. B gave Duke a nod before walking away toward the direction of his mate.

Duke sat down on the cave floor next to the Fae. He didn't turn to look at the man, but instead watched his Mad Dog teammates. The three that had yet to return felt like a gaping hole in his vision. He couldn't feel them like the rest of the Mad Dogs, but he did feel their absence.

"They're shifters, aren't they?" Mac asked.

The Fae's question caught Duke off guard. Not because of the question itself, but because the question made it obvious the Fae didn't know the answer. The question also told Duke that this Fae had not been in their world long if he hadn't learned how to identify a shifter. Duke was just about to reply when his earbud was flooded by Doc's voice.

"Coming in hot!"

Chapter Nine

Doc never sensed anyone when he started back toward the cave. He carried Paul and Hunter trotted, even with his limp, at his side while they ascended the ravine toward the cave. The first shot made him tense, but not duck or drop Paul. The second shot had him ordering Hunter to get his ass to the cave. He was promptly told 'fuck you' and Doc couldn't help but mentally chuckle. He had thought the same thing when Oh gave the same order more times than he could count, so he really couldn't be bothered that Hunter's reply was the same.

Several shots were aimed at them. The bullets that ricocheted off the rocks made Doc think that either the assholes were shit shots or ordered not to kill them. Not killing them made sense if the shooters were rogue councilmembers' mercenaries since if they had sided with Shanna or Donovan, they would want to take a Mad Dog alive.

Even though they didn't know about Doc's new ability, he was sure the rogue councilmember fuckers would be happy with *any* Mad Dog if for no other reason than to try and trade them for M or B. If not both. Of course, if it was the Organization shooting at them then they were just shit shots since those fucker's only wanted to take out the Mad Dogs.

Return fire came from the direction of the cave and Doc wasn't surprised his pack was covering their ass.

The gunfire that chased them up the ravine seemed to lessen. There was a clear distinction of three shooters. So, when suddenly those three became two, Doc was sure one of his unit took out at least one of the assholes firing on him, Paul, and Hunter.

H and Gabe were moving down the rocky terrain toward Doc and their two pack mates who were in wolf form. Doc was running as was Hunter at his side even though he was limping while bullets pinged off the ground around them.

Gabe and H returned fire to give their pack mates more cover. Neither Mad Dog could see the hostiles that were trying to kill their pack mates. They didn't give a shit though as they fired down the mountain.

B and M weren't far behind H and Gabe. However, they didn't head down the mountain. Instead, they perched just outside the cave and brought their sniper rifles up in an attempt to find targets. Jordy crashed down next to M at the same time his husband, Nick, assumed the spotter position next to B. Two scopes, or in this case four, were always better to find assholes to take out. None of the Mad Dogs who looked through scopes, sniper or spotter, found anything to shoot.

Duke disappeared, but none of the Mad Dogs noticed their vampire teammate vanish into thin air. The only one who witnessed Duke react to the sudden assault on the cave was Mac. One moment the vampire sat on the cave floor next to him and the next, he stood and disappeared.

The soldier in Mac reacted without any thought that he was surrounded by nonhumans who could easily hurt him if they wished. He pushed up from the wall and took the four steps that would bring him to where his weapon lay next to the comm man. Mac ran toward the cave entrance. He gave no thought to the seemingly passive comm man. Maybe he should have because the body that threw him off course hit hard enough that he dropped the weapon he'd barely grasped. The next thing Mac knew he was pinned down under the only Delta unit member he thought was human.

Rowan startled when the patrol leader appeared at his side and picked up his weapon. He'd watched his teammates treat the man as if he were a threat. So, he acted accordingly. A flex of his legs launched him up from his semi kneeling position and slammed his body into the rearmed soldier. Rowan may not know why the Mad Dogs suddenly treated the man as if he were a prisoner, but he had no doubt they had their reasons. It was his faith in those reasons that made him react and ensure the patrol leader wasn't going to be armed and pointing a weapon at his teammates back. Especially, while they were engaged in a firefight outside the mouth of the cave.

"Stay the fuck down," Rowan growled as he secured the patrol leader into a position that would prevent him from getting up.

"I just want to help," Mac pointed out. "I'm no threat to your team. Let me help."

Rowan didn't even need to think of his answer. "The Mad Dogs can handle it."

Mac was securely pinned under the Delta soldier. It didn't matter that the man restraining him was human. Of course, Mac could just teleport to gain his freedom, but if he did any trust he'd already gained would be lost. So, instead he just relaxed under the human while the sound of gunfire reached their ears.

Doc passed H and Gabe with Hunter hot on his heels. Thoughts of how he would explain a wolf running at his side while he cradled one in his arms when he reached the cave where the furthest thing from Doc's mind as he trotted through the entrance. Jordy and Nick stood when he reached M and B's position. They fell in step behind him with no thought to the danger of being shot that they'd put themselves in, but his teammates actions only registered in Doc's subconscious.

Shots outside the cave entrance told Doc that the team was still engaging whoever the hell was firing on him. His mind set on the rapid sound of gunfire. He was so focused on the Mad Dogs current engagement he barely registered Jordy taking Paul from his arms. The gunfire petered out before Doc could even contemplate a plan to go on the offensive or even request a SITREP from his pack who had been providing them cover.

Doc pressed the mic it his throat. "Report."

All he felt from his mate and across the pack link was pure focus to take out the assholes who threatened them. He knew from those feelings his pack wasn't injured, but he still needed an update on what the hell just went down.

"Suppressed," H replied. "Heading back."

Doc could see the rest of his pack so he didn't hide the relief he felt when H checked in and confirmed he and Gabe were on their way back. He knew his pack would feel his relief. He also knew they would feel his remaining concern underlying that relief. Duke wasn't in the cave and he hadn't replied when Doc ordered his teammates who were present to report.

"Duke," Doc called to their vampire teammate.

It didn't matter that B no longer required Duke to restrain him from killing someone when he fed. No, Duke was a Mad Dog even if he wasn't, couldn't become, pack. Silence greeted Doc. He couldn't feel Duke across their pack link and the vampire's lack of reply made the hairs on the back of Doc's neck stand on end.

"Duke," Doc tried again and still received no response.

"Rowan." Doc turned to order Rowan to contact HQ and noticed the born wolf who was part of their unit sprawled on top of the patrol leader. Not just sprawled, but pinning the man down so he couldn't move.

Doc had no idea what to make of the scene he was seeing. His confusion must have flooded the pack link because Gabe spoke.

"Duke said he was Fae," Gabe informed Doc, but the wolf's explanation sounded more like a question than an answer to the confusion they all felt from Doc.

Doc looked away from where Rowan pinned Mac down to take in the rest of the cave. The two humans from the patrol were still laid out along the wall. Their eyes were wide and bouncing from the team to the wolves while they pressed as close to the cave wall as possible. Doc was sure they would have bolted out of the cave if their path wasn't blocked by several Mad Dogs.

His pack was scattered around. H and Gabe had their backs to him as they stood sentry at the mouth of the cave. Jordy stood sentinel after he'd set Paul down near the cave wall and several feet away from the injured patrol soldiers. Hunter lay almost curled around Paul, and Doc knew the closeness would benefit both men while in wolf form.

M, B, and Nick still stood at the cave entrance. They didn't face him, but stood sideways as if waiting to spin on a dime to engage an enemy again. The only team member who was missing was Duke.

"Duke, report," Doc ordered again after pushing the mic at his throat.

Tension filled the pack link as the Mad Dogs waited for their teammate to reply. There was no reply.

"Rowan," Doc addressed his new teammate. "Get off him and call HQ. I want to know where Duke is. Now."

Rowan almost didn't recognize the gentle laid-back team leader he'd come to know because of the seriousness of his tone. So, he scrambled off the patrol leader so fast he gave no thought to the man he'd been restraining or that he might be a threat to the unit. Seconds after Rowan reached the comm pack; he had the handset in hand and was waiting for HQ to answer his call.

Mac didn't move off of the cave floor where the wolf restrained him. He had no idea what to expect from the shifter Delta unit that apparently included a vampire. The last thing he wanted was for them to think he was a threat. He wasn't. Mac understood they could hurt him if they wanted to. Sure, he could teleport away, but he was still too young to have anything more defensive in his arsenal. And, he sure as shit didn't have anything offensively that could allow him to fight back if the nonhuman Delta unit decided to actually hurt him.

For the first time since he'd left home, he wished he'd stayed there longer instead of indulging his desire to be around humans. Remaining passive was his best bet for survival. It was also the best bet to ensure his two remaining patrol members would get the medical attention they needed. Mac didn't think the Delta soldiers would harm the humans he'd been responsible for, but if they let him attend his men he'd feel better regardless. All of this he thought as he watched the Delta leader assess their current situation.

Doug wasn't really sure what he was seeing on the big screen attached to the wall when he looked over the top of his monitor. He watched the heat signatures move across the screen and it was obvious that his team was engaging an enemy.

However, he didn't try to contact the team, his new pack, because he didn't want to distract them. Still, that didn't mean he wasn't tracking every red dot he labeled with a pack member's name. Well, he also paid closer attention to the heat signatures which belonged to Rowan and Duke. They may not be pack, but they were Mad Dogs so he paid their heat signatures just as much attention. It was this attention that showed Duke's heat signature, which he still didn't understand since vampires didn't put off heat, blip from the center of the others at their base to a location behind several enemies that appeared to be following Doc, Paul, and Hunter.

Doug didn't give Duke's 'dot' much thought. The vampire's movements during the team's last engagement were just as exact. Even when it seemed the vampire was in the midst and surrounded by heat signatures, which Doug knew were the enemy, he didn't give Duke's 'dot' much thought. Until…

"Mad Dogs, HQ."

"HQ, Mad Dogs, go ahead," Doug replied to the familiar voice of his friend, Rowan.

"Requesting location of Duke." Rowan's tone made the hairs on the back of Doug's neck stand on end.

The sudden request for his vampire teammate made Doug realize the vampire wasn't just attacking their enemies on his own. Something was wrong.

Doug took a steadying breath before he replied, "sending you the coordinates now."

Doug tapped on the keyboard and understood their satellite connection would give Rowan Duke's location in a matter of moments. However, the coordinates for the location of their vampire teammate weren't enough Intel for the unit.

"Mad Dogs, seven hostiles are showing with Duke. They are moving northwest. Currently four clicks from your location."

Silence greeted Doug and he held his breath while he waited for Rowan to confirm the Intel he'd shared. He felt helpless. There wasn't shit he could do other than what he'd already done: give the Mad Dogs information to succeed with their mission.

"Copy, HQ," Rowan finally replied. "Mad Dogs out."

There was nothing more Doug could say or do to help the unit. So, he stared at the screen on the wall that displayed the heat signatures of his teammates, his pack mates, and the names he'd assigned to them days ago.

Doc listened to Rowan give him an update from HQ. He had his shields locked down tight because he didn't want his pack to feel his worry over Duke. It was more than obvious Duke had been captured by whoever the hell had been shooting at him, Paul, and Hunter.

Doc was more than sure the gunfire that had chased them up the ravine was lessened because of Duke's intervention. He was also sure Duke's actions were exactly what resulted in the vampire's capture. Doc had no doubt Duke was now in enemy hands.

What he wasn't sure of was which one of their enemies actually had Duke. It could be the Organization or the rogue Councilmembers' mercenaries. He wasn't sure which faction would be worse, either, but as to who took Duke was neither here nor there. Someone took a Mad Dog and they would pay. No one took a Mad Dog, whether they were pack or not. They would get Duke back. Doc understood he wasn't the only one who would be determined to make that happen once he shared the Intel with the rest of the team.

However, before he shared that Intel, Doc had to address the revelation of the patrol leader. The only Fae Doc had ever had any interaction with was Councilwoman Carmen aside from Shanna Crystal. He could admit he didn't know shit about them aside from their ability to disappear and create portals. He knew even less about what they were capable of because the unit had yet to spend any time with their new Councilwoman.

It was because of this that Doc kept his guard up when he approached the patrol leader. Doc could feel his pack tense in preparation to attack if needed, but Doc tried to ignore the feeling that flooded the pack link.

Mac lay on the cave floor where Rowan left him. Doc wasn't sure what to make of the Fae's passiveness and lack of movement. He didn't think the Fae was playing 'possum', but the man's passiveness was almost unnerving after seeing him be so dominant while controlling his men.

"Sit up," Doc ordered.

Mac had been observing the large Delta team leader since the moment the man stumbled into the cave carrying a black and gray wolf in his arms. It didn't escape his notice that a large black wolf limped into the cave next to the Delta soldier, either. Mac ignored the wolf that was handed off to another of the Delta soldiers. He also ignored how both wolves curled around one another once they were settled along a cave wall only a few feet from his men. However, Mac was sure the wolves were no threat to them.

"You are Fae," Doc stated instead of asked once Mac sat up.

"I am," Mac confirmed and didn't hide the pride he had for his kind when he replied.

"They don't know?" Doc squatted down in front of Mac.

"No," Mac replied. "No reason for my men to know. It wouldn't change my leadership in their eyes and even if I thought it would..." Mac paused before he raised a brow. "Do you really think they would believe 'fairies' are real?"

Doc couldn't help but smirk. Humans loved to read about werewolves, vampires, fairies, and a bunch of other shit, but subconsciously they knew it was just fiction regardless of how many of them wished it was not. The knowledge that humans thought they possessed, conscious or not, was the only thing which kept them all safe. If it weren't for doubt and more strongly their disbelief, all of the non-human races would be screwed.

"I'm not sure what to do with you," Doc admitted unabashedly. "Your men are no threat to us nor in any position to cause us trouble. You on the other hand," Doc let his sentence trail off.

"I am not a threat to your pack," Mac began to correct himself. "To your team. I give you my word."

The way Mac said the last along with the slight sensation of the hair on Doc's arms standing as if suddenly exposed to static made him believe there was more than just words to Mac's promise.

"Let me help you retrieve your teammate." Mac purposely didn't refer to the missing Mad Dog as a vampire. Even though they were speaking in a whisper, he didn't want to alarm his men any further. Seeing them watch the two wolves with fear in their eyes was bad enough.

Doc didn't know enough about Fae to make a decision. He would rectify that in a moment.

"Tend to your men. Explain about us and yourself." Doc met Mac's deep green gaze steadily. "Leave Duke out of it."

"They won't be able to return to the human world if I do that." Mac frowned and his tone was full of concern.

"Do they have family? Spouses or kids?" Doc asked even though the answer really wasn't going to change his order. The humans had been exposed to their world and the longer they were around, the less chance Duke could make them forget what they've seen without causing them serious damage either physically or mentally.

"No," Mac replied and clearly understood why the Delta team leader was asking.

"Then you have your orders." Doc stood and walked over to where Rowan still squatted by the comm pack. "You are with me. Bring the pack."

Rowan nodded and they both stood before heading toward the tunnel at the back of the cave. Several feet into the darkness, Doc stopped. Rowan bumped into him and Doc put a hand out behind him to steady the man. A moment later, Doc cracked a glow stick and shook it until it glowed brightly before he dropped it between them onto the tunnel floor.

"Get HQ on the line," Doc ordered and they both knelt down with the pack between them. "I need to speak to O'Tool."

Rowan's only reply was a nod before he picked up the cradle and did as he was ordered.

Chapter Ten

"Go ahead, Mad Dogs," Doug acknowledged the call.

"I need O'Tool on the line."

Doug hid his concern when Doc replied instead of Rowan. "Standby."

Doug slapped the red button for the second time in so many days. Moments later the CO, his second, and even Chuck barreled through the door to the comm room.

"SITREP," Oh ordered from Doug as he put a headset on.

"Another encounter with hostiles and Duke has been separated from the unit," Doug informed and nodded to the large monitor on the wall.

Oh frowned over at the screen. He clearly saw Duke well away from the team, but even as he watched, Duke's dot disappeared. At first, he thought Doc may have been checking in to inform them of Duke's possible capture, but now he wasn't so sure.

"Go ahead, Doc."

"One of the patrol, the leader, is Fae," Doc didn't waste any time informing Oh of the situation. "I need more information on Fae before I can determine what to do with him." Doc paused, but remained keyed up. "Also, the remaining two humans have been exposed to us and Duke has likely been captured so we need updated coordinates for him."

"Shit," Oh cursed to the men around him. He had no idea which cluster fuck to address first so he decided to go with the easiest to handle of the three. "We just lost GPS on Duke. Doug will send you his last known coords," Oh informed Doc. "I'll contact the councilwoman to get Intel on your Fae soldier."

"Advise on humans," Doc requested.

"Your call, but you need to recruit," Oh reminded and ignored seeing Chuck tense in his peripheral vision. Regardless of how the civilian felt or what he thought about how they became Mad Dogs was no concern to Oh. He didn't give a shit.

"Okay, Oh. GPS on Duke's last coords just came through. Mad Dogs out."

Oh didn't reply before Doc disconnected the call. He removed his headset and turned to Doug. "Keep me updated if anything else develops."

"Yes sir," Doug replied and turned back to his monitor. He didn't say a word to Chuck who took up his workstation next to him.

El watched his mate while they walked back to Oh's new office. He fully expected Oh to be pissed at the current development. So, he was surprised that he only felt calm concerned-laced determination through their link without even needing to send those emotions to his mate.

Oh entered his office. For once it didn't even cross his mind that the office used to belong to McCormick, but he didn't notice. Instead, he walked directly to the slightly glowing stone the councilwoman left them so they could contact her.

He had no idea how the damn magical stone worked, aside from needing to touch it. He also didn't know what to expect, either. So, he braced himself for anything when he placed the palm of his hand on the rock. A low, vibrating, hum filled the office. Oh looked at his mate when nothing else seemed to happen after a few minutes. El hadn't even finished shrugging when Councilwoman Carmen appeared in the office behind his mate.

El felt his mate tense through their link at the same time he felt the presence of someone behind him. The hum had disappeared at the same time, so El felt he was safe to assume the person he sensed was the councilwoman. He turned around slowly and was proved correct.

"Good afternoon, Oh," Councilwoman Carmen greeted and stepped further into the office from where she appeared in the doorway. "El," she acknowledged with a dip of her head to the Mad Dogs second in command.

The Fae Council representative still made Oh feel off balance. Whether it was because he and the rest of the Mad Dogs were so accustom to interacting with Rolex for so many years, or just because they didn't know her well, Oh didn't know. Probably both, but those thoughts could be pondered another time.

"I was not expecting a mission update so soon." Carmen smiled. "May I sit?"

Once more, Oh felt thrown off balance. The councilwoman acting as if they were equals or even friends was not something he thought he'd ever get used to. Granted, Rolex had behaved the same way toward the Dogs, but he had *been* a Mad Dog. Not only a Mad Dog, but a pack mate with him and McCormick.

The councilwoman was standing next to the chair across from his desk and Oh realized she was still waiting for his permission to sit.

"Yes, of course." Oh nodded and took his seat behind the desk. Once the councilwoman was seated, Oh began. "We are not finished with the mission. The team has run into some complications."

"What can I do to help?" Carmen asked sincerely.

"We need information," Oh replied honestly and hoped the only Fae they knew since dealing with Shanna Crystal would share information about her species.

"I'll give you what I can." Carmen smiled and Oh believed her.

So, he gave her a rundown of everything Doc had told them. Her face remained neutral except when he mentioned Duke's capture. She appeared unhappily shocked at that information. Oh could relate. He was surprised the vampire had been captured as well. The mention of the Fae patrol leader brought a totally different expression to her face and noble bearing. She frowned and tensed. Her reaction to this Intel made him and his mate tense, as well, as if they could feel her in their link.

"I see." Carmen nodded after he'd updated her.

"Is he a threat to the Dogs?" Oh couldn't keep the protective growl out of his question.

"Doubtful," Carmen replied. "If he's been serving in the US military, there is little chance he is a threat to the unit."

"But?" Oh demanded and felt his anger rise at not knowing enough about her species.

"There is no way to be sure until I meet him," Carmen said so neutrally she sounded as if she and the Fae were just going to have tea or some shit.

"You're going to Afghanistan?" El asked and understood the surprise he felt in their link was not only his own.

"Yes. It is the only way to be sure." Carmen stood. "So, please excuse me."

Neither Oh nor El had a chance to make a reply before their Council representative blinked out of existence before their eyes.

Mac knelt next to his two remaining teammates. Cash and Stick weren't too injured considering the shit they had all been through. Cash's arm was in a sling and Stick's shoulder was bandaged from where he'd been shot. Scrapes and bruises covered them as well, but they were walking wounded and would survive. Well, physically anyway if they followed him back into the supernatural world Mac had left behind years ago. Mentally, he wasn't sure and tried not to think about which outcome would be preferable.

Neither of his teammates looked at him, but instead they both continued to stare at the two wolves across from them in the cave. Mac had deduced that the wolves were the Delta soldiers Hunter and Paul, though he wasn't sure who was which wolf.

"How are you guys holding up?" Mac met the eyes of both his men.

Cash's eyes flickered over to him then back to the wolves before he answered. "Not too good LT. I think I'm seeing shit that I know can't be there."

"I'm seeing it, too," Stick whispered. "Kinda freaking me out."

"Look at me," Mac ordered. "They ain't gonna hurt you."

Cash glanced at him again. "You see them, to?" He sounded almost hopeful.

"Yeah, Cash, I see them," Mac confirmed. "They are really there. You're not hallucinating."

At his declaration both Cash and Stick looked at him. Their matching wide-eyed stare would have been comical in any other situation. Sadly, their expressions weren't the least bit funny right now.

"There are some things I need to tell you, but I don't want you to freak out," Mac started.

"Like why there are wolves in Afghanistan?" Cash asked at the same time Stick said, "Too late for that, LT."

"Yeah, Cash." Mac nodded. "But you need to know you are safe. You're not in any danger from what I'm about to tell you."

Mac really didn't want to expose his men, his human men, to the world they knew nothing about. Hell, the world they were better off knowing nothing about, but he had no choice in the matter. He had his orders, but even if the Delta team leader and pack alpha hadn't ordered him to tell Cash and Stick about their hidden world, Mac would have to if for no other reason than these were his men and they'd been exposed.

He could wait for the vampire to be rescued and have him wipe their minds, but that would likely cause them more mental damage than if he just let them think they were experiencing some joint PTSD hallucination. He respected his men too much to do either, especially since he had the option to explain the reality they now found themselves in. Still, Mac wished his men hadn't been thrust into this situation.

"You're not making me feel any better, LT," Stick said as his gaze shifted back to the wolves.

"I doubt what I'm gonna tell you will either," Mac replied grimly and sat on the cave floor next to Cash.

"Just lay it on us straight, LT," Cash requested. "You've never led us wrong or lied to us about shit."

Mac forced himself not to wince. Cash was right in that he'd never led the men he was responsible for astray. However, he had been lying to them from day one. Telling humans about fairies, and that he was one, was just something that wasn't done. Hopefully, his men would understand.

"They are werewolves," Mac spit out the information quickly. No buildup or speech about the supernatural world. No, just an info dump like ripping off a Band-Aid.

"What?" Stick exclaimed loudly enough that his question echoed throughout the cave.

Mac didn't think Stick's light brown eyes could grow any wider or his pale skin go any paler. He was wrong when his man stared at him open mouthed. Cash just continued to stare at him and Mac wasn't sure what to make of his silence and suddenly scrutinizing gaze.

"They won't hurt you," Mac reassured Stick again. "You're not in any danger."

"You don't know that," Stick protested and pushed himself further back against the cave wall as if he could disappear into it.

Cash was still staring at him when Mac replied, "they wouldn't..." Cash interrupted quietly, "he does know." Stick's gaze whipped away from Mac's deep green eyes to look incredulously at his teammate.

Mac never broke the steady stare that Cash leveled on him. Cash's expression was that of focused neutrality and Mac hated that his normally so expressive teammate felt the need to suddenly repress what he felt. Mac was sure Cash wasn't afraid. He'd seen the man set his jaw and fight his way through his fear when they'd been in the thick of an engagement with an enemy. No, Cash's jaw wasn't set now and his body wasn't tense as it normally would be before engaging an enemy.

Stick on the other hand was clearly freaking out. His eyes were wide and they darted between Mac and the wolves while his breathing picked up to the point Mac felt the eyes of several of the wolves looking in their direction. He had no doubt they could not only hear Stick's increased breathing, but every word he said to his men. Mac didn't care. No, all he really cared about, at the moment anyway, was his men.

"Stick. Look at me." Mac grabbed his teammate by the back of the neck and forced the man to look at him. "You. Are. Safe. You are. Fine." Mac waited for Stick to nod before he pulled back. "Yes, I did know," Mac confirmed Cash's statement without looking away from Stick. "But not until we got back here after our failed attempt to get to the EZ."

"Are you one of them?" Cash asked before Mac could finish. Mac tried not to be hurt by Stick flinching away.

"No. I'm not a werewolf." Mac met Cash's steady gaze once more.

Cash was quiet for a moment. When he finally spoke, Mac wasn't surprised by what he had to say. "But, your *something*," Cash said with certainty.

"Yes. I'm Fae," Mac admitted and waited for the fall out his admission was sure to cause.

"What the hell is that?" Stick asked with less fear in his voice Mac had heard since he joined his men on the cave floor to have this discussion.

At the same time Stick spoke, Cash laughed loudly as if he'd heard the funniest joke ever. Mac was well aware that his eyes were as wide as saucers. The last reaction he ever expected from Cash was laughter.

"You're a fairy," Cash managed to say through his laughter. "That is appropriate." Every one of his men knew he was gay.

"A fairy." Stick looked from Mac to Cash and back again. "Like with wings? Wings that flitter fly?"

Cash roared louder with laughter at Stick's question. So loud that Mac was sure they were still the focus of everyone in the cave. Even the two wolves looked over at them. Mac was sure if wolves could form an expression on their face it would be one that displayed they thought the three of them were crazy. Cash was still wiping the tears from his eyes and still chuckling at Mac when Mac continued.

"Yes, but no wings. I am one of two races of Fae, but that's not what's important right now."

"Oh, I beg to differ." A soft feminine voice declared from the entrance of the cave.

Mac cursed himself. He had been so focused on his men that he never sensed the Seelie who suddenly now occupied the cave with them.

Doc was just as surprised to see their councilwoman in their Afghanistan cave as the rest of his pack. He felt their surprise and forced his own down so he could instead send them calm. After he spoke to Oh, he expected his old team leader to gather the Intel he requested and call them back. He never expected to step out of the tunnel and suddenly see the councilwoman appear after he took in the position of his men.

Mac was where he'd ordered the man to be and Doc, hell even Rowan, had no problem hearing the humans reactions to what Mac shared with them even though he and Rowan were still trudging up the tunnel. Paul and Hunter were still snuggled up together in their wolf forms while the rest of the Mad Dogs hadn't moved from their positions where they had been stationed before he and Rowan entered the tunnel.

Thankfully, his pack was trained well enough they just didn't open fire when anything happened that surprise the hell out of them. The sound of the comm pack beeping and Rowan answering registered even though Doc didn't stop looking between Mac and Councilwoman Carmen.

"It's the CO," Rowan said softly and nudged Doc with the handset.

Doc accepted it without taking his eyes away from the potential problem that could result in the two Fae confronting one another. He just didn't know what to expect since he really didn't know shit about Fae.

"Go ahead," Doc said after he blindly accepted the handset.

"Councilwoman Carmen…" Oh began.

"Is here," Doc cut off his old team leader and handed the receiver back to Rowan without another word.

He tuned out Rowan as he finished talking to Oh while he stepped more directly into the cave. Mac still hadn't replied to the councilwoman and his only perceivable movement was the tensing of his body. Mac's men both sobered from their amusement and fear caused them to tense as well. However, they still stared at their LT as if waiting for the order to attack or defend if needed. Neither man's expression gave the impression they couldn't do either just because they were injured.

"This is an unexpected surprise, Councilwoman," Doc addressed the Fae that was now their intermediary with the Council. "My request for information wasn't intended to mean we needed you here." Doc stepped up to the smaller Fae woman. "Unless of course you feel you needed to be here."

Doc knew the councilwoman understood exactly what he was implying. Just the fact that she was here at all after he requested Oh for information on Fae made Doc question his instinct and judgment where the patrol leader was concerned. However, he kept his expression neutral and his emotions of self-doubt firmly behind his shields.

"Good afternoon, Alpha," Carmen greeted him with a nod and a smile. "I know this is an unprecedented situation, but after your CO made his request I felt it best to assess the situation myself."

The councilwoman continued to smile as her gaze roamed over the cave and took in everything. Just seeing her standing serenely in her black slacks, pale button-down blouse, and high heels in an Afghan cave was beyond weird for Doc. He was sure the rest of the pack felt the same. If she were Rolex, they would know how to react, but she wasn't. Of course, if she were Rolex she wouldn't have appeared out of nowhere, either.

Councilwoman Carmen closed the few steps between them before she spoke again. "Your pack is in no danger, Alpha." She patted his arm and stepped around him to face Mac.

"Let us talk, young one," Carmen said and her tone clearly indicated she was still smiling and fully in charge of the situation.

Mac knelt forward and was about to stand when Cash reached over Stick and grabbed his forearm. The intense concern and almost pleading for an order gaze the man leveled on him told Mac that his men still stood behind him even after everything he'd told them. There was still more, a hell of a lot more, to share with them, but just knowing they still had his back like he had theirs made him proud to call them brothers-in-arms.

"Everything is fine," Mac told Cash without breaking eye contact. "She is Fae and obviously affiliated with the Delta wolves." Mac ignored Stick mouthing 'Delta wolves' and continued. "You're both safe here." Mac looked between his two remaining team members. "Don't forget that." Mac grinned. "I'll be back soon."

Mac pulled out of Cash's grip when he stood. He turned and finally laid his eyes on the powerful Seelie female he felt standing behind him. She wasn't the first Seelie he'd ever seen. No, that would have been... Mac pushed the thought of his former lover away. However, she looked nothing like he expected. She wasn't in her true form, but neither was he. Still, the last thing he expected to see was a smartly dressed business woman who looked like she should be sitting in a board room instead of standing in a dirty cave in Afghanistan.

Mac had no doubt he hid his surprise at her appearance before she noticed. However, his gaze never left hers when he approached. He stopped the proper distance away from her as one would when interacting with an elder of their kind. Seelie or Unseelie, the court protocols and decorum were the same. Mac greeted her by pressing his flat palm over his heart before touching his left ear with two fingers then his lips with the same two fingers.

"Feel nothing but peace and love, listen and hear honesty, speak nothing but truth to be heard."

The Fae woman greeted him the same way in return and Mac tried not to exhale a breath in relief. Not all Fae, light or dark, followed court protocol. It was those that didn't abide by the social norms of the Fae society that Mac not only worried about, but in his experience caused so much trouble and discord they had to be put down to protect their individual courts and societies.

"I am..." Those were the only words Doc understood when Councilwoman Carmen introduced herself to Mac after their alien greeting. He didn't understand Mac's reply, but it was clear the Fae had exchanged their names in their native language. Doc watched as the councilwoman turned sideways and stretched her arm out in an invitation for Mac to lead the way out of the cave. Mac nodded to her before he walked out of the cave with her following.

Should we follow them? H asked and Doc wasn't surprised his mate suggested such a thing.

No, they will be fine, Doc replied to his mate's mental inquiry.

"M, B," Doc keyed up the mic at his throat. "Keep your eyes on the terrain surrounding the councilwoman and patrol leader. I'm sure they can take care of themselves, but just in case."

Doc wasn't sure of any such thing or he wouldn't have ordered his sniper teammates to keep watch. They may have known that as well, but said nothing other than to confirm the order.

"Rowan," Doc called out to his only non-pack Mad Dog and looked in the man's direction. "Sit with Mac's team and let me know if HQ calls again."

Rowan nodded and followed his order, but not before Doc caught the man's curious and questioning look.

Chapter Eleven

Rowan's gaze was following the patrol leader and the woman who was associated with the Mad Dogs somehow as they left the cave when Doc spoke. His team leader gave him the order to 'sit' with Mac's patrol mates. Rowan understood why Doc issued that particular order. He was the only non-Mad Dog in the cave aside from the two injured men. Rowan wasn't exactly sure what Doc wanted him to do. Maybe Doc just wanted him to comfort them since their team leader was now disappearing with a business-looking woman. Or, maybe Doc wanted him to reassure them that none of the Mad Dogs were a threat and wouldn't cause them any harm.

He didn't know, didn't have a clue, but this wasn't the first order he'd follow in which he was oblivious of the reason he'd been told to do something. Rowan stopped next to the injured patrolman and dropped the comm pack before he sat and leaned against the wall.

"Linden, Money," Rowan addressed them by the name on their uniforms and nodded to each man respectfully. "I'm Knox, but everyone just calls me Rowan and I prefer it that way."

Rowan didn't attempt to shake their hands. He didn't need to be a Mad Dog, part of their pack, he corrected since he *was* a Mad Dog, to recognize the vibe their body language was screaming at him. Both soldiers were tense. No surprise there. Hell, the world as they knew it was fucked and Rowan couldn't expect them not to be freaked out. Linden's eyes were still wide and held a hint of fear. Money on the other hand, was tense, but his gaze was full of scrutiny more than anything else.

"Cash," money finally said and stuck out his hand to shake. Rowan did just that. "This is Stick," Cash indicated his fellow soldier.

"I can see that." Rowan grinned and held his hand out to Linden. The man hesitated to take his hand and it wasn't until Cash shoulder pumped him that he actually did.

Before a weird silence could even settle between them, Cash spoke, "are you like them?"

Rowan followed the direction Cash nodded toward to indicate Hunter and Paul. An unexpected surge of jealousy surged and Rowan had to stomp it down.

"No, I'm…" Rowan started to reply, but Cash interrupted.

"Like the LT?" Cash raised a curious brow.

"Um, no. I'm just a shifter," Rowan replied with the human equivalent word for garoul quickly in case Cash attempted to interrupt him again. Several minutes passed and Rowan tried not to feel like a bug under a microscope as he held Cash's gaze.

"*Just* a shifter?" Cash asked with a raised brow. "What does that mean? You're not a wolf, but something else?"

Rowan continued to hold Cash's chocolate brown eyed stare. The man's gaze was one of curious caution, but Rowan didn't sense or scent any fear rolling off the soldier. No, that smell only came from Stick, even if it did seem to be lessening.

"I'm a wolf. A born wolf," Rowan replied with pride. "But only a Mad Dog because I am part of this unit."

Cash frowned and Rowan had no doubt he confused the man on several levels with his admission. So, he let the man think. He'd answer whatever question Cash threw at him first. He didn't have to wait long.

"You said 'born' so, what does that mean?" Cash asked in a tone that held more curiosity than his expression showed.

"There are two types of shifters, apparently," Rowan began. "Those of us who are born and those like the Mad Dogs that are turned. We never knew anyone could be made a shifter until we met the Mad Dogs," Rowan finished almost absently.

"We?" Cash asked and pulled Rowan away from his thoughts of how he and his original pack mates were so surprised, shit shocked, that such a notion existed.

"Those of us who were born shifters," Rowan answered honestly. "Apparently, the Mad Dogs never knew we existed so the surprise was mutural."

"Born," Cash repeated, but Rowan knew it wasn't a question so he waited for the soldier to speak again. "The Mad Dogs, your unit?" Rowan nodded. "They were human once?"

"Yeah, though I don't know anything about how they went from human to wolf," Rowan answered honestly even though he sure as hell knew how someone human or shifter became a Mad Dog.

"Are they going to make us like you?" Stick finally spoke.

Rowan couldn't determine if it was fear or something else he heard in the human's tone. Regardless, it wouldn't have changed his reply.

"Not unless you want them to." Rowan met Stick's gaze steadily. "I'm a shifter but not a Mad Dog in anything other than name."

"Why?" Cash asked before Rowan could elaborate.

Rowan was tempted to tell the humans about Chuck and everything he felt toward his best friend, the wolf he loves, and how Chuck's feelings about him going through what was needed to be done to become a Mad Dog was the only thing stopping him from joining this pack. Not only joining this pack, but becoming a full member of the unit. He was tempted, but he kept all of his personal bullshit drama to himself.

"I'm just not ready yet. I'm still part of the unit even if I'm not a part of the pack," Rowan finally answered and watched Cash absorb his explanation.

Rowan could see the wheels turning in Cash's eyes. The man suspected he wasn't telling him everything, but Rowan was okay with that. His personal shit was just that: personal.

"Wait," Stick said and looked between him and Cash. "So, we can choose to become a werewolf? Like some American werewolf in London shit?" Rowan bit his tongue over the reference to the American classic and just nodded his head affirmative. "What if we don't want to be one? They are going to kill us if not, right? They can't let us live now that we know about them. Oh fuck!"

Stick rambled and looked at Cash fearfully as if begging his teammate to tell him this was all a dream and if not; tell him what they were supposed to do.

"Calm down, Stick." Cash put a hand on his teammate's leg and Rowan noticed the soldier visibly settle down.

"No one is going to kill you, Stick," Rowan assured the human and was 99% confident in his assurance. "Though," Rowan continued and met Stick's light brown eyed gaze. "There is a war we are fighting and you are a soldier. The Mad Dogs are a military unit and we need soldiers to fight this war," Rowan declared with confidence. "The war we fight isn't a human one, but it's actually more important because it could change humanity as you know it. I'm not telling you this to change your mind. This is no bullshit."

Rowan only paused to meet each soldiers' gaze head-on. "Mad Dog, shifter, human, or something else like your LT, there is a war going on. So, the Mad Dogs won't *force* you to do anything, but I know they need and would welcome a few more good men," Rowan finished his speech. A speech he never intended to give, but gave nonetheless.

He waited for Cash to comment since that was the human Rowan knew absorbed information and asked pointed questions. Cash remained silent and Rowan wasn't sure if Stick did as well because the beanpole soldier was following his teammate's lead. It didn't matter to Rowan why both humans decided to clam up. They would speak and ask their questions when they were ready. Rowan would be sitting next to them when that time came. Unless of course, his team leader ordered him to be somewhere else.

Mac followed the female Fae who was clearly his elder out of the cave. The female's business casual attire barely registered with him since the weight of her age pressed against him so strongly. Whatever he thought he might do where the werewolves were concerned was suddenly a moot point now that he was in the presence of such a powerful Seelie.

It wasn't just the difference in their age or the fact that she was Seelie, from the court of light, and he was Unseelie from the dark court, that made Mac understand instinctively he was her inferior. He could feel the Seelie's power and it was strong. Very strong.

Mac was a baby Fae in terms of their species and he knew this, which was exactly why he continued to follow the elder without saying a word. Of course, he didn't need to say anything to stop the plethora of thoughts that bombarded his mind.

He had only encountered two Seelie Fae before, one of which was his only lover, so he had no experience to fall back on when it came to this female. He also had no experience interacting with a Fae so much older than he. Several meters to the west of the cave entrance the woman stopped. Mac would have been surprised, shocked even, that she could traverse the rocky terrain in high heels if he had not known she was Fae.

"This will suit us fine," Councilwoman Carmen said with a smile and indicated several boulders that surrounded them. "Let us sit," she suggested, but Mac recognized it for the order that it was.

Mac just tilted his head in deference to the older Fae. He wasn't sure where this meeting with the woman who was obviously invested in the werewolf unit was going to go, but he wasn't about to offend the Seelie elder. So, he perched on one of the larger boulders she indicated.

The woman leaned against another large boulder across from him. Mac waited for her to speak. When she did, it was in the human tongue of English. Mac was almost relieved he wouldn't need to converse in the Fae native language. He hadn't spoken his native tongue in so long that even the greeting he offered the Seelie felt foreign when it passed his lips.

"You have found yourself in a situation," she started and her smile never left her face.

"One I never wished to find myself in," Mac spoke freely. "I just wish to live in the human world and help make it a better place without revealing our kind."

Mac never broke eye contact with his kinsmen even if they were from opposite sides of the Fae realm. All Fae were related, one way or another.

"You are young," Carmen replied candidly even though her words stated the obvious. "And now you are placed in a situation that you never could have prepared for. Tell me, young one," Carmen paused. "How strongly are you tied to this human realm?"

Mac didn't even blink in surprise at the elder's question. He didn't pause before answering, either. "This is where I have made my home. I am Unseelie, but this is the realm in which I choose to reside," Mac paused and only continued at the Seelie's raised brow prompting. "I've given my promise to the alpha wolf that I would not harm his pack or unit."

Mac watched the female nod approvingly for his decision to give his pledge to the werewolves. Still, whether she seemed pleased or not he wasn't going to harm the wolves, not that he actually could even if he wanted to, Mac wasn't sure what else the Fae elder from the Seelie court wanted from him.

"You are aware of the war they are engaged in?"

"No, not really," Mac answered honestly.

"You have been in the human world for a long time," she said almost passively. "Time here isn't as it is at home."

"I know this," Mac interrupted.

"Time isn't the only thing that is different in this human realm," she paused. "We've always remained hidden. Hug the shadows or blended in seamlessly with humans who didn't know to even question our existence."

Mac continued to meet her pale eyed gaze and didn't interrupt the elder again who was speaking to him.

"That is not the case any longer. There are factions that strive to reveal more, reveal all that have remained hidden in plain sight of the humans. It is this which is the war the wolves fight."

Mac didn't need the Seelie elder to spell out things for him. If the wolves or anyone else in the supernatural world were suddenly exposed to humans then they all were in jeopardy. Mac had remained hidden in the human realm and was perfectly content to live as one of them. The human realm was his refuge. Now, it seemed like that refuge was going to be ripped from him as if someone was pulling a rug out from beneath his feet.

"What I need to know, young one, is if you will join these wolves to fight this war."

He had already given his word, his promise to the Delta team leader, so there was no question how he would reply to the elder Seelie.

"I've already given my promise to the Delta team leader who is the wolf pack alpha that I would assist them," Mac informed the beautiful face seated on a boulder across from him.

"Your word is your bond as it is with us all," she said. "The word you gave the alpha was before you knew the entirety of the situation."

Mac attempted to interrupt, but the elder held up her hand to stop him. Protocol dictated he concede to her wish that he remained silent.

"You are not bound to this war even though you gave the alpha your promise. Should you wish to leave and take your humans with you, I nor the wolves, shall stop you." Once more she paused before she continued, "however, you may be young, but I am sure you are old enough to understand the potential consequences of your humans' exposure to our world."

"My word is my bond as it is with us all," Mac replied echoing her words without hesitation. "My men have been exposed to a world they would have been better knowing nothing about, and there is nothing that can be done to change that. I am confident they will not only keep our world secret, but join this war to defeat those who threaten to expose us all."

Mac wasn't sure where the hell the words he'd just spouted came from. He wasn't even sure if he believed them, but after he made his declaration, he would force himself to believe them until they became true. He maintained eye contact with the elder Fae woman. She had stopped smiling at some point, but now after his near outburst defending his men, she smiled widely.

"I have no doubt the Mad Dogs Alpha will appreciate you joining the cause. However, the choice to actually *become* a Mad Dog will be yours. Yours and the humans you lead."

Mac frowned in confusion and was about to speak the moment the elder Fae stopped. He never got the chance because the moment the last word left her mouth, she teleported away. Mac wasn't disturbed by her sudden disappearance. No, he was used to his kind: Unseelie or Seelie, just disappearing into thin air. Still, that didn't mean he was okay with the elder just up and disappearing after giving him such a cryptic reply.

Mac rubbed the frown lines between his brows. He had no idea what she meant when she claimed it was his choice and his remaining teammates to become a Mad Dog. He knew the Delta unit was called Mad Dogs. However, the way the Seelie said Mad Dogs made Mac think there was more to those words than just a unit's designation.

It was obvious the Delta team were a pack. Well, obvious once Mac realized what they were. What wasn't so obvious was how the vampire fit into a wolf pack. Mac had only encountered three vampires after he decided to make the human realm his home. Two of the three encounters were nothing more than accidental paths crossing. The other was definitely not accidental. No, not accidental, but totally enjoyable. Three days' worth of enjoyment over and over again.

Mac gave himself a mental shake. Now was not the time to be thinking of the incredible sex he'd had with the last vampire that crossed his path. No, now is the time to speak to the Mad Dogs alpha. He may have already given his word to the wolf that he wouldn't escape or hurt any of the soldiers under the man's command, but he had yet to give his full pledge to join the fight, the war, the Delta wolves were battling. He had every intention to do just that when he returned to the cave.

None of the werewolves stopped him when he approached and eventually entered the cave. A quick sweep of the space showed the Mad Dogs' team leader talking to the elder Fae woman who had disappeared from in front of him less than three minutes ago. Another one of the Delta soldiers was sitting with his men.

Mac had to tamp down the sudden flood of protectiveness that raced through his veins. There was no reason for it, but just seeing one of the wolves so close to Cash and Stick made him feel like a mama bear that needed to protect her cubs. Slowly, Mac walked toward his men. They seemed relaxed, considering everything he'd shared with them before the elder Fae woman appeared. So, he pushed his protective impulse down and changed course to walk directly to the alpha wolf and Fae elder.

"I shall have a portal for you when you call for one," she said.

"Thank you," the alpha replied before she disappeared again.

Mac undersood the team leader had to be relieved to hear they had a quick escape when the time came. The wolf's expression didn't display that relief, but a good team leader's wouldn't.

A gasp from the direction of his men made Mac turn toward them. He gave Cash and Stick a reassuring smile and tried to ignore the sudden expressions of nervousness and shock displayed on their faces. Mac had a lot of explaining to do and he only hoped his men would understand his deception. He also hoped they wouldn't look or treat him differently now although he was sure there was no way they wouldn't.

"Councilwoman Carmen explained what your promise or pledge means."

Mac refocused on the alpha wolf when the man spoke. "Then allow me to formally give it to you," Mac requested.

The alpha raised his hand to stop Mac. "I release you from your pledge to me and my pack."

"What?" Mac asked with confusion, since the statement was the exact opposite of his intention.

"Before you give your pledge, you need to be fully aware of the war you are committing to."

"The elder explained it to me already," Mac interrupted.

"You also have to speak to your men," the alpha finished as if Mac hadn't spoken.

Mac turned to look at Cash and Stick. The shock at seeing the elder Fae disappear before their eyes seemed to have faded. The wolf next to them was speaking to them and Mac was sure whatever he was saying had everything to do with his men's behavior.

"I pledge until my dying breath to fight this war by the Mad Dogs side. I pledge to protect any Mad Dogs life on or off the field of combat and follow all orders given to me by my team leader and the pack alpha. This is my pledge as it is freely given," Max said before the alpha could say anything more.

The wolf frowned at him as Mac felt his pledge settle in his heart and mind. The sensation was only slightly painful, but the pain didn't last more than three breaths.

"I'll see to my men," Mac informed, but it came out as permission to do so. The alpha wolf only nodded before he turned away and walked to the cave entrance.

Chapter Twelve

Doc wasn't happy when he approached M, B, and the born shifters who were being trained to be his future snipers. There was no doubt his pack mates felt his emotion through their pack link because Doc didn't bother to shield them from how he currently felt.

Doc? H's voice whispered in his mind.

I'm fine, Doc replied to his bond mate.

Okay.

Doc was fully aware H didn't believe him for a second. The sense of calm support that flooded Doc from his mate and the rest of the pack told him as much.

"M, take B, Gabe, and Rowan to find Duke," Doc ordered. "You have his last coords. Kill anything that gets in your way, but I want at least one alive so we can get Intel. We don't know which faction might have him, but I don't give a shit about that. Whoever might have him can give us Intel regardless of who they are fighting for."

"Roger that," M nodded. "Who do you want shifted?"

"That's your call," Doc informed. "They are your team."

M frowned. He had been a team leader before he became a Mad Dog and was aware the pack was going to be split into two teams when they returned to Camp Smokey. Still, he didn't expect Doc to implement the split while they were on this mission and he sure as hell didn't need to like it.

"Alright," M begrudgingly accepted his new promotion to team leader. "If I'm taking Rowan with the comm pack, how will you keep HQ updated?"

"Hunter will keep me apprised of your status and you will need to keep HQ updated more than I," Doc informed. "Contact HQ for extraction once you have Duke. Councilwoman Carmen already knows our location and can extract us after you have Duke."

"Okay." M nodded once, before he pressed the mic at his throat to order Gabe back to the cave.

Once Gabe arrived, Doc ordered, "Mad Dogs move out." It wasn't lost on him when he walked back into the cave that he parroted the order Oh issued to them over the last thirty-four years.

"B, give your gear to Nick," M ordered his mate. "All of it, then shift."

B started to undress after he handed his sniper rifle to Nick. He was almost fully naked when Rowan joined them. B ignored the glances directed at him from Rowan, he was sure the man was trying to hide. He ignored the flare of lust that filled Gabe's brown eyes, as well, even if the wolf remained soldier focused. B shifted into his tan and gray wolf the second his last piece of clothing hit the ground.

"We have a Mad Dog to retrieve, so move out," M ordered and mentally told his bond mate the direction to get them one step closer to finding their vampire teammate.

Doc stopped just far enough in the cave to be obscured by shadows. He easily heard M speaking to his team. It felt odd. Doc also felt a loss that was unfounded, but he was sure to keep that emotion firmly locked behind his shields.

He had total faith in M and his pack mate's ability to lead a team. Still, that didn't stop him from watching his pack mates until they disappeared from his view into the rocky terrain.

Mac sat with his arms on his bent knees in front of Cash and Stick. Cash observed him with curiosity and Stick watched him with guarded nervousness. In fact, Stick looked more nervous now than when the Delta wolf sat with them.

"I'm the same man you've known for the last three years. I hope you won't forget that," Mac started. "I know you have questions. I'm going to answer every last one of them. So, hit me."

For the next hour, Mac answered their questions. Most were focused on him. Why he came here to live with humans, what his home was like, the differences between Seelie and Unseelie, and more along that vein until they picked his brain on werewolves. Mac told them what he knew of the shifters, but admitted there was much he didn't know.

"This war Rowan spoke of," Cash continued to meet Mac's gaze. "We are joining it, right?"

"They can use all the help they can get since they are fighting on two fronts," Mac started. "But it's your choice."

"You're joining them, though," Cash said with confidence.

"I am, but you don't have to," Mac repeated even though he had no idea what he would do if they decided to stay out of his world.

A vampire might not be able to erase their memories after being exposed to the reality of the world they actually lived in, but Mac was sure someone could do something that didn't involve the soldiers' deaths.

"We will follow you, LT," Stick said with conviction.

Mac hid his surprise that it was Stick who committed them to this war and not Cash. Stick had asked him very pointed questions and Mac didn't miss the fact that the man relaxed more and more as he answered. Still…

"Cash?" Mac asked his Sergeant.

Cash snorted with a smirk. "As if you need to ask."

"I'm going to be honest," Mac glanced between his patrol mates, but was interrupted by Cash.

"You always are, LT."

"I'm not sure what this will mean for you." Mac once more looked at both of them seriously. "I don't know any humans who are aware of my world."

"Our world," Stick interjected.

All Mac could do was smile at his men. "I also don't know what it means to be part of a werewolf unit. They are a pack, so I don't know if we would need to be as well, or even how that would happen since we aren't wolves."

"We will figure it out," Cash stated. "If we can become part of their pack, we will. If not, we will at least be in their unit to help kill the motherfuckers who are threatening our new world."

It didn't escape Mac's notice that this was the second time his men referred to the supernatural community as their world and not just his. He loved the hell out of them both before and even more so, now.

Mac was sure the wolves in the cave had been listening to his conversation with his men. In fact, it would have been practically impossible for them not to hear. They were werewolves after all. Still, that didn't stop Mac from looking over his shoulder toward the alpha wolf that was squatted next to his two shifted teammates. The alpha met his gaze and gave him a slight nod. Mac returned the nod before turning back to his men.

"So, let me tell you what I know about vampires," Mac began and shifted his weight to get more comfortable before resuming his soldiers' education on another species in his world.

Their world, Mac mentally corrected himself with a grin before he started to speak again.

"This is Duke's last known location," M informed Gabe and Rowan. "Spread out and see what we can find."

He had no need to tell his mate what to do. B was already working the area in ever widening circles. His nose was to the ground and he only occasionally raised his head into the wind. M understood his mate wasn't checking the wind for any scent of Duke. No, he was scenting the wind to ensure they weren't caught unaware if hostiles decided to attack.

"Got something," Gabe said as he stood. In his hand he held Duke's comm equipment and wrist GPS unit.

M walked over to Gabe. He trusted Rowan and B to cover their position while he and Gabe examined the items that would have made finding Duke a piece of cake. The GPS unit was smashed all to shit and all that was left of Duke's throat mic was small pieces of plastic dangling from his earwig wire.

"Shit," M cursed and put Duke's equipment into one of his flak jacket pockets. "B, update Hunter."

His mate never looked up from where he was trying to find a trace of Duke's scent on the ground, but M had no doubt B was updating Hunter on their find. Still, M watched his mate for several moments before he spoke again.

"Can you feel him, B?"

No, B replied mentally to M's question. *Haven't really been able to feel him since my feeding has been under control.*

M was aware of the weakening of his mate's link with Duke, but he didn't think it would hurt to ask.

"Got something else," Gabe informed.

M turned back to Gabe. He'd been aware his pack mate had moved off to continue searching the ground. M's gaze narrowed on the yellow and red fletching's of a tranquilizer dart Gabe held. He wasn't surprised to hear B's low growl behind him while he approached Gabe.

Just the sight of the dart pulled up memories of when they were on R&R. M was sure the same memories were pushing to the forefront of his mate's mind, too. At least they knew who they were dealing with now. Well, that wasn't totally true, but they at least knew who'd grabbed Duke.

M took the dart from Gabe and wasn't surprised to see the slight glazed-eyed look in his eyes. Gabe was accessing the Mad Dogs' memories and M didn't miss when Gabe found the one related to the dart. Even had a deep growl not rumbled in Gabe's throat, the anger that flooded their pack link was more than enough to let them know how the wolf felt.

"Rowan, get HQ online," M ordered without looking at the man. "B, update Hunter."

"Mad Dogs, HQ," Rowan said into the handset attached to the comm pack.

"HQ, go ahead Mad Dogs," Chuck's voice replied and Rowan squashed his warring emotions toward his best friend.

"HQ on the line," Rowan told M and handed him the handset.

"We have verified the Council or their mercenaries have Duke," M informed. "We need a detailed scan of our position."

Less than three minutes later, Chuck spoke again. "Roughly six heat signatures to the northeast of you. I am sending the coordinates now."

"Mad Dogs out," M said the minute the GPS unit's screen on his forearm lit up. M handed the handset back to Rowan before he addressed his mate. *Northeast, B.*

B nodded and jogged by his mate to lead the team in their new direction. The feel of Marcus' gloved hand running across his back when he passed felt good, but he wasn't distracted by his mate's touch. No, it just registered as pleasant when he passed since his full attention was on finding a scent trail that would lead them to the assholes who had taken his Sire.

B caught the scent of a necromancer a click and a half from the last location where they found Duke's equipment. *I've got a necro scent,* B informed M and waited for his mate and the rest of the team to catch up to him.

"B has scented a necro," M informed the team. "They must have a mage or Fae if they didn't leave any scent between here and where we found Duke's stuff."

"As long as we don't end up dead, they aren't hard to take out." Gabe grinned.

"Spread out," M ordered. "Find them, B."

B nodded to his mate and resumed his northeast trek to follow the foul scent of death the necromancer left in their wake. Less than twenty minutes later, he stopped.

Voices ahead, B informed and M immediately held up a fist to stop the team's forward movement.

"Voices ahead," M whispered into the mic at his throat.

None of the wolves replied, but every one of them cocked their heads to listen. Their hearing was enhanced in their human form, but still not as acute as their wolves'.

Take us close enough to hear, B, M told his mate who was now hunched down almost flat against the rocky ground.

Slowly, B moved closer to the voices until he could finally hear what they were actually saying.

"Taking this piece of shit was a waste of time. They don't want the vamp. They want one of those fucking military werewolves," a deep voice said angrily. "If Samson wasn't such a shit shot, we would have had one by now!"

"Well, he's dead now so it doesn't matter," a second voice replied.

"Asshole deserved it even if this shit ripped his neck out," the first voice replied before B heard the distinct sound of flesh being hit.

B bit back a yelp that almost escaped his muzzle when a sharp pain shot through his underbelly. It felt as if he were the one who was kicked and it happened so suddenly that he had no time to shield the feeling.

"What was that?" Gabe whispered to the team.

They could all see B, so they knew he hadn't suddenly become injured even though the pain M and Gabe felt through the pack link indicated otherwise.

B? M inquired with a tone that indicated he was asking as their team leader and not just the man's mate.

"He did, but if you didn't trash the shit he was wearing, we could at least have monitored their movement and set a trap," the second voice sounded just as pissed as the first.

"They will come for him," a female voice assured.

"Son of a bitch," M cursed under his breath. He felt anger and confusion in the link he shared with his mate and Gabe.

"What is it?" Rowan whispered quietly and M was sure he'd feel concerned curiosity from the lone wolf who wasn't part of their pack if the wolf was actually a part of the link the pack shared.

Lucy, B confirmed what M was sure he'd already known.

"We've encountered this necromancer before," M whispered to the rest of the team. "Her name is Lucy."

M sent the memories of Lucy being part of the mercenary unit that had captured him and B to Gabe. He also sent how she'd help them escape. Gabe's shocked gasp was low across their comms, but was quickly followed in their link by an anger that bordered on rage.

"And you didn't kill her?" Rowan asked softly.

M mentally cursed again. If Rowan were a Mad Dog, he'd have seen the same memories M just sent to Gabe. "It was conducive not to at the time," M replied to Rowan. "This time it won't be conducive at all. That bitch will die today."

Anger joined B and Gabe's in their pack link and M had no doubt Rowan heard it in his tone even though he couldn't feel it firsthand. "Slow and steady. We kill everyone who is not Duke," M ordered and gave no thought to his ignoring Doc's order to take some alive. He mentally sent the same instructions to his mate.

They were just rounding a bend in a rock formation when B was hit with so much pain; he had no choice but to yelp. At the same time a net landed on his back and gunfire erupted. The team took cover behind what scarce boulders they could find.

"Fuck!" Gabe cursed, no longer trying to keep his voice quiet.

M felt pain in their link the second before Gabe cursed. "How bad?"

"Through and through. My shoulder," Gabe replied. "That fucker is going to pay for this shit."

The anger in the link from Gabe was enough to tell M the wolf was still combat fit even if he was injured. Still, that didn't stop M from issuing his next order. "Rowan, get to Gabe. I'll give you cover."

"Copy," Rowan replied and moved to follow the order the moment M started to lay down suppressing fire.

Two of the four men who were trying to drag B's net incased body went down. M wasn't sure if it was he or Gabe, maybe both who took them out and really didn't give a shit. All he cared about was getting his extremely pissed off and snarling mate free of the net.

The remaining two men trying to drag B away went down and he doubled his effort to get free of the net. The remaining men held AK's, but held their guns as if the Mad Dogs weren't minutes from killing them. B could see a collapsed body on the ground several meters ahead of him. It was clearly Duke. Standing next to his Sire, was Lucy and another man.

Stupid fucks, B thought when he sent the image to his mate. He snarled at the men and that bitch, Lucy. All she did was grin. Her grin was the last thing he saw before pain like he'd never felt before racked his body and his world went dark.

M felt B's pain and his connection in the pack link dim before it almost disappeared completely. The feeling was so close to what he'd felt when they had been captured that had he not been able to see his mate still trapped by the net, he would have thought their link broken again. However, that didn't stop the scream that tore from his throat which turned into a low and resonating growling howl throughout the ravine as if death itself had joined the fight.

M didn't feel his clothes shred, his boots split, or the strap of his rifle snap when he shifted into his third form. No, all he felt was the consuming rage filling the void where his bondmate's presence should be strong instead of barely discernible. Vengeance toward those who were responsible wasn't even a stray thought, it was a given when bounded ahead.

"Holy shit," Gabe muttered at seeing his team leader in this form for only a second time before he started laying down suppressive fire.

Rowan was frozen. He had no idea what he was seeing and the vision locked his brain up as if his head was suddenly a prison in which he had no room to move. Distantly, he heard gunfire but it barely registered under the terrifying growls that came from the beast that could only be their team leader.

Gabe realized his weapon was the only one he heard. He glanced at Rowan. He easily recognized the shell-shocked expression and frozen body of a soldier whose mind had shut down.

"Rowan!" Gabe yelled at his former pack mate.

It was hard to concentrate and continue to give M cover fire while the rage that filled their pack link threatened to bring him to his knees and he tried to snap Rowan's mind back into action. However, Gabe pushed through it all. He needed Rowan, especially when two of the three men standing next to the woman began to fire on M.

"Rowan!" Gabe tried again and moved closer to his old pack mate. Gabe couldn't afford to look away from where M was charging toward the net that shrouded his mate who was still in wolf form. Still, that didn't stop him from shoulder bumping Rowan hard enough to stagger the man.

"Rowan!" Gabe yelled again and was relieved to hear the sound of gunfire begin to join his.

Gabe's angry voice calling his name and the jolt of being jostled enough he had to catch his balance or fall snapped Rowan out of his shocked stupor. Gunfire swarmed back into his ears with a rush and it shattered the silent tunnel his mind had placed him in. Gabe broke him free from his stupor just in time to see two bullets rip into the beast that was their team leader. Rowan didn't know what M was, but he did know the wolf was his teammate. Not just his teammate, but his team leader. That knowledge was enough for his training to kick in without any conscious thought.

Gabe mentally breathed a great sigh of relief when Rowan finally joined the firefight and they each took out a man who was firing on them. He was more than sure seeing M in this form was horrifying for Rowan. Hell, if Gabe hadn't seen M's current form back at Camp Smokey, he'd be horrified as well. In fact, he was still somewhat from just seeing the wolf in action. However, now was not the time to consider his feelings about their team leader. He could dissect them later because right now was the time to ensure they all survived this encounter.

Chapter Thirteen

Duke was only conscious enough to feel pain and his child being close. He'd killed five of the mercenaries before he felt several stings in various places on his body. He remembered the sensation immediately from when he helped the Mad Dogs while they were on R&R. He'd been tranquilized then by one dart. His system was able to shake off the effects that shouldn't have been able to affect him at all. This time, four darts, he couldn't do anything but succumb to the lethargic sensation that ensured he'd be more than pliable for his captors. And he was.

Still, his inability to defend himself, let alone escape, didn't stop his captors from beating on him. His captors were mercenaries hired by the Mad Dogs rogue councilmembers. Of that, he was more than sure when in a moment of lucidity, he recognized the necromancer Lucy from after he betrayed his organization, the Watchers, and his Sire.

Duke didn't have a single regret when it came to helping the military werewolf unit rescue M and B in South America. No, as he cracked his eyes open to see his surroundings at the first sound of gunfire; he only regretted the sight of his child's still body under a net several meters from him. He could still feel B, so Duke knew he wasn't dead. However, as he watched his child, the fact that B was unconscious was confirmed when he morphed back into his human form.

The desire to help his child and the burning need to protect him was tearing at Duke's mind and body. His body felt like a lead weight and as unmovable as freight train whose wheels were locked up. All Duke could manage with the control he barely held on to by a thread was to crack his eyelids partially open and watch the scene before him unfold. He did just that and knew if he could smile, he would as he watched Marcus in a rage he'd only seen twice before where his mate was concerned. It didn't matter that Duke was the reason for one of those times. No, all that mattered now was that Marcus would save his mate, Duke's child, one way or the other, even if it killed the Mad Dog.

Marcus didn't feel the pain of the several bullets he was aware had hit his body. There wasn't room for pain to take root in his fury. Rage was all he felt as his world turned into a long tunnel that ended with Lucy and another man standing over Duke. However, no thought was given to his vampire teammate. Not that M didn't care for his teammate. He did, but his fury, his rage at barely feeling his bond mate through their link overrode his concern for anything or anyone other than B.

His mate was unconscious and the two people in his sight were responsible. They would pay. The howl that escaped his muzzle sounded more like a lion's roar when he leapt toward Lucy and the man.

He slammed into a barrier. A clear shield like barrier which he hit hard enough he felt his left wrist snap like a twig and caused him to shake his head to clear the spots that suddenly filled his vision. Another howl tore from his throat and he swiped at the invisible shield that protected the bitch and asshole who M wanted to shred limb from limb.

"What a bad little puppy you are," Lucy cooed with a smirk.

M growled at her and couldn't help being pleased that the man next to her began to look concerned when M changed tactics to break the shield. He never took his golden glowing gaze away from the man as he began to drag his claws along the shield while he walked.

Surprisingly, his three-inch claws actually screeched along the shield as if he were dragging them down a chalkboard. M lifted his muzzle and inhaled deeply. The shield connected to rock four feet to the right side of where both the fuckers were standing next to Duke. M didn't even bother to turn around to determine the extent of the shield on the other side of the rogue councilmember mercenaries. No, he just started walking backwards, claws scratching the invisible shield and filling the area with the spine-chilling noise and his growls.

The shield didn't extend as far to the other side of the mercenaries. However, it was the shortest distance on the left side of the shield that would have made him smile if his shifted face could display such an expression. There was a scent of fear from the man and the stench of death from Lucy that all necromancers exuded when they went on the defensive. If he could smell them, then the shield wasn't a bubble. It was a wall and walls could be scaled. Once more, he wished he had the ability to smile.

Gabe never took his eyes off their team leader. From the corner of his eye, it was clear Rowan hadn't either as they approached B. Rowan looked scared shitless and Gabe really couldn't blame his old pack mate. Still, as long as Rowan was combat fit, even temporarily, Gabe would take it.

He had already reached out to Hunter to give the older wolf an update on their status. He hoped the wolf didn't hear the relief in his tone while he gave his report. It was the relief he felt at knowing they weren't out of range of the rest of the unit.

Gabe placed himself near where B was still lying unconscious under the net. He could hear Rowan behind him muttering, but paid the wolf no mind. There was no way to let M know they had reached B other than to have Hunter tell their team leader. So, that's exactly what he did. Gabe knew his message was received when M turned his head and began walking their way.

Rowan had dropped the communications pack and didn't give a shit about the equipment. He had to force himself to focus on B. His teammate didn't display any physical injuries. Not even a head wound that could explain his current state of unconsciousness.

Maybe it's the net, Rowan speculated to himself.

Rowan retrieved his K-Bar with a swift movement that was more muscle memory than from practice. Just as swiftly he was slicing the netting away from his teammate. He paused in pushing the netting off of B when he caught movement in his peripheral vision. Rowan trusted Gabe to cover him while he tended to B, but that still didn't stop him from looking away from B and glancing through Gabe's spread legs.

Rowan wished he hadn't when he witnessed the beast that used to be their team leader. He froze once more. Both his human side and wolf understood the way to survive a predator was to freeze in hopes they wouldn't be seen. So, that was exactly what Rowan did and he didn't breathe again until the beast pivoted between one blink and another. He charged back toward where their vampire teammate was slumped on the ground between his captors.

Hunter's voice in his mind informing him Gabe and Rowan had his bondmate was enough for M to turn away from the shield. He would have had to move away from the shield to execute his plan of attack anyway. The attack was still going to happen, but he wanted to make sure his mate was safe, along with the rest of his team.

M's golden gaze met Gabe's and his new pack mate's brown eyes held raw anger. M understood Gabe could feel his rage since he didn't shield his emotions, but his new pack mate was adding his own level of pissed off to their pack link.

Gabe radiated no fear. Not in his body language or scent. Rowan on the other hand was terrified. The soldier froze still as a statue when their eyes met and the scent of Rowan's fear was heavy on the slight breeze that moved through the ravine. Rowan's fear of him would be addressed later. Right now, M planned to face Lucy and the man next to her. Mid step, he spun and was moving.

M wasn't aiming for the shield when he leapt this time. Instead, he aimed for the rock face to the left of where the mercenaries bracketed Duke. One clawed foot pushed into the flat shield before he pushed himself higher. His right hand slammed into the rock face and he shoved off it and spun. M had no idea if he could propel himself high enough to clear the top of the shield wall, so he prepared for another jarring impact if his uninjured hand didn't grasp the lip of the shield. His feet pushed off the rock face and his clawed hands felt nothing but air.

The death curdling screams of both Lucy and the man when they realized their shield was now worthless echoed off the surrounding rocks. M landed half on Lucy and his massive weight took her straight to the ground. Claws tore into her body while his jaws locked firmly on her throat. The damage from his front and back claw tipped paws caused her was inconsequential when he shook his head. Three shakes were all it took before her head tore loose from her body. M gave no thought to where it landed or the foul taste of the necro in his mouth.

In fact, even the nauseating stench of death she exuded defensively didn't register. His sole focus was on the man who had scrambled several feet away from where he torn Lucy nearly limb from limb. To say the mercenary was as pale as a sheet would have been an understatement. M didn't give a shit about how all the blood seem to flee the man's skin when he leapt off Lucy's corpse and over Duke's prone body toward the second target of his rage. He could practically already taste the man's blood in his mouth while he tore him to pieces.

That taste never came to fruition. M felt one of his claws tear into the mercenary, then the ground was beneath his paws and his jaw snapping on nothing but air. He spun quickly seeking his target, but the man was gone. Seemingly disappearing into thin air, but that didn't stop M from tilting his head back in an effort to catch the asshole's scent. Nothing. The only scents that filled his nose were those of Lucy's torn apart body, lilacs and fresh turned earth from Duke, and his teammates who were several yards away. M's failure to execute his attack on the second target of his wrath filled him with fury once more. His only outlet for it was his voice, he howled long and hard.

"M."

M finally lowered his head and swiveled toward the sound of his name being nervously called. He had no idea how many times Gabe had said his name or how long his new teammate had been trying to get his attention. However, now that he focused on his pack mate, he could feel the calm the wolf was trying to send him through their link.

"M," Gabe repeated again and didn't look away from his team leader's golden eyes. Still, Gabe stood far enough away he would have plenty of time to raise his rifle and pull the trigger if he needed to, but he understood a few more bullets in M's body wouldn't do shit to save his ass if M wanted him dead. Gabe waited for a better indication than just meeting M's gaze before he spoke again. When M tilted his head to the side to indicate he was listening, Gabe did just that.

"This." Gabe waved a hand to indicate M's whole body. "Is some bad ass shit. But Rowan needs to get to Duke and he's scared shitless of you right now. How about shifting one way or the other so he can get in there?"

M growled and was impressed when Gabe stood his ground. His growl was one of frustration at not being able to communicate with Gabe. The current level of adrenaline coursing through his veins wasn't going to allow him to shift one way or the other at this time. So instead, he just gave Gabe a nod and started to circle wide of where Rowan was still crouched by his mate. It never even registered in his mind that the shield seemed to have disappeared with the mercenary who escaped.

Rowan froze mid movement while he returned something to the med pack. M hated that the wolf felt like prey because of him. No wolf was ever prey. M gave Rowan a nod and stopped his advance toward his bond mate. He was sure if the bond link he shared with Gabe hadn't returned to its normal strength, M wouldn't have even considered Rowan's fear before rushing to his mate's side.

Rowan still hadn't moved. Hell, M wasn't even sure if the wolf blinked since they locked eyes. So, he glanced at Gabe before turning back to Rowan and moving his head to indicate the wolf should join their teammate. He would have pointed to indicate his order, but was sure pulling Rowan's attention to his long ass claws would only make matters worse.

"Rowan, c'mon. Duke needs attention."

Gabe's voice seemed to break Rowan out of his fear induced state. He scrambled up and grabbed the med pack before running over to where Gabe stood next to Duke. Rowan purposely didn't look back over his shoulder to watch his team leader. He didn't have to because he knew the beast that was M would be at B's side.

Duke still had trouble opening his eyes and keeping them open for any length of time. He was getting snapshots of what was happening around him. Rowan was leaning over him, touching him, and he could see one of the new Mad Dogs standing sentry just over the medic's shoulder. His hearing was just fine and he was grateful the wolf was talking to him, explaining to him what he was doing.

A groan escaped his throat when a bright light was shined in first one then his other eye. The light didn't cause him any pain. It was just bright as fuck. He would have swatted Rowan's hand away, but his body still felt like a lead weight. Duke wasn't too worried about his inability to move at the moment. No, he was too relieved to feel his child again and just as relieved to see Marcus' hulking form squatted down next to Brian.

B, Marcus called out to his mate across their link.

B looked physically unharmed even if something had happened to cause him to go unconscious. His mate was curled up in a fetal position, but his breath was strong and steady

B. Marcus tried again and reached out a clawed paw to brush strands of his mate's light brown hair back from where it had fallen on his face.

M? Brian replied to the voice in his mind that sounded like his mate.

I'm here, B.

Brian tried to open his eyes. He was only successful enough to catch a glimpse of his mate. M was shifted into his third form and squatted next to him. Just seeing his bondmate sent a flood of relief through him.

I feel heavy, M, B told him. *Like I am too heavy to move.*

Marcus had seen B's eyes briefly flutter open before his mate spoke. He glanced over his shoulder and could see Duke still lying on the ground. Duke and B were connected. They had all learned that the hard way when his mate tried to kill himself. So, Marcus felt safe assuming that B's current state had something to do with whatever happened to Duke which caused the vampire to still be immobile.

You're going to be fine, B. We just need…

Marcus' voice and his mind cut off abruptly and turned into a vicious growl that filled his ears. Brian forced his eyes open a crack and could now only see one of his mate's fur covered legs. He couldn't see what had caused Marcus to now be standing over him and issuing warning growls that B easily recognized.

If Gabe hadn't been watching M with B, he never would have reacted as fast as he had. The second he witnessed the flex of his team leader's fur covered legs, he raised his rifle. He didn't need a target to be ready to kill. Gabe felt Rowan move behind him and had full confidence the wolf was now kneeling and ready to protect Duke if the shit hit the fan.

A portal appeared several meters behind M and B. Gabe was moving to flank without thought. He didn't even stop when he heard Rowan speak.

"Comm pack is beeping," Rowan said loud enough for the team to hear even though he never took his eyes off the portal that suddenly appeared.

Gabe finally stopped before getting into position. "Hunter says 'don't shoot the Councilwoman'. So, I guess we should expect…"

"Yes, you should, but I am reassured to see you are prepared for anything that may appear." Councilwoman Carmen stepped out of the portal a moment later.

She was dressed, once more, in a smart business suit more suited for a board room or in her case a council chamber than the Afghan mountains. Her makeup was flawless and her red lips spread in a serene smile.

"It's time to go home."

Councilwoman Carmen stepped to the side of the portal so smoothly it was like she was wearing combat boots instead of four-inch heels. How she didn't trip on the rocky terrain was beyond all the Mad Dogs, but not really at the forefront of their minds at the moment.

M glanced at the rest of his team and his only acknowledgment of the Councilwoman's words was to step to the side so he was no longer looming over his mate. He gently bent and picked up B before settling his bondmate comfortably in his arms and against his chest.

Gabe watched their team leader gently cradle his mate. M looked at where he stood half the distance between the portal and where Rowan knelt at the ready by Duke's side. M gave him a nod to indicate he return to Rowan and help him with Duke. Gabe returned the nod and jogged back to Rowan.

"I'll get him," Gabe informed Rowan. "Go get your gear." He nodded toward where Rowan had dropped the comm pack.

"Alright," Rowan replied and didn't turn away until he was sure Gabe held Duke over his shoulder securely.

He only managed one step before he froze again at the sight of their team leader. For several moments he stared at M and took in the sight of this hulking beast holding their fragile looking teammate so gently in his arms. It was this visual as well as the soft almost passive gaze of M's glowing golden eyes that broke Rowan out of his current fear. He slowly walked over to where he'd dropped the comm pack on the ground next to B and picked it up.

Rowan's eyes never left M's and he was relieved when their team leader stepped back and nodded toward the portal. A quick glance around the area showed the bloody remains of a body, but no sign of his other teammate. So, with only a quick look over his shoulder which revealed their team leader hadn't moved an inch, Rowan stepped through the portal.

"Your work, I am sure." Councilwoman Carmen commented with surety as M walked toward the portal she had created to take them home. Marcus couldn't reply and she knew this, but also was sure she wasn't expecting one. "I look forward to your report."

Marcus grunted by way of a reply and stepped through the portal. He fully expected to feel the Councilwoman's presence behind him, but he didn't. So, he looked over his shoulder and found the portal was gone. She didn't follow his team to Camp Smokey. Marcus didn't care or even concern himself as to where the Councilwoman went because right now, he needed to get his mate to the med center.

Chapter Fourteen

Chuck was watching the monitor. The moment the red dots which represented the unit and patrol soldiers started to blink out, he panicked. His hand hovered over the red button he was beginning to hate. However, before he had the chance to press it, Chuck picked up the sound of two sets of boots marching down the hall outside the comm center. He bolted out of his chair and ran out the door. Chuck was talking before he even stopped in the hall.

"Sir, the team… they just disappeared," he panted out and tried to get a grasp on his panic. "They were there, both groups, and then they just started to disappear one by one."

"Calm down, Chuck," Oh ordered gruffly. "They are fine."

"But, Sir," Chuck interrupted. "They are gone! I don't know where they went. We need to find them!"

Chuck recognized he was yelling at the CO of the Mad Dogs, but he didn't care. The team, Rowan, was gone and they needed to locate them because he refused to think they were all dead.

"They. Are. Fine," Oh bellowed and ignored the calm he felt his mate pushing into their bond link. He also ignored El's gentle reminder in his mind that Chuck was a civilian.

Both Oh and El felt the moment their old pack mates returned to Camp Smokey. Doc and H were determined while M was concerned. B was in their link, but his emotions were muted. That was enough to tell them both that B was injured in some fashion. However, M's lack of panic told them B's injuries couldn't be bad, though.

Chuck stared at the CO's outburst. He had heard the wolf use that tone before, but it had never been directed at him. In fact, the tone made Chuck instinctively take a step back from the alpha wolf.

"They are back!" Doug shouted through the doors that lead outside.

Chuck just blinked stupidly while his brain absorbed Doug's announcement. It wasn't until Doug disappeared back out the doors and all he saw was the backs of the CO and his second stepping outside that he snapped out of his stupor.

They are back, A relieved Chuck mentally repeated Doug's announcement. *Rowan is back.*

Chuck was moving before he even finished his thought. He expected to see some level of chaos when he stepped outside since he was already aware that some of the team and patrol soldiers suffered injuries. However, that wasn't the case.

Two of the Mad Dogs were in wolf form and he deduced they were Paul and Hunter just by scanning the team. Gabe carried the vampire over his shoulder and Marcus, in his scary ass beast form, was carrying Brian. It was also obvious that two of the three patrol soldiers were injured, judging by the bandages they sported and the way they were walking.

That was all Chuck took in before his eyes, with laser focus, settled on Rowan. His best friend appeared unharmed. So much so, Rowan didn't even glance toward where Chuck stood next to the CO and his second.

"Doc," Oh called out to his former pack mate and the current Mad Dogs Alpha. "SITREP."

Doc glanced back over his shoulder. He wasn't happy Oh wanted to be updated on the mission before he even had his wounded situated in the Med Center. So, he didn't bother to hide his displeasure when he changed course to walk toward his previous team leader. Still, that didn't stop him from issuing orders on his way.

"Rowan," Doc paused long enough to meet the wolf's gaze. "With H. He will show you how to take care of our wounded. Gabe, show Mac where he and his team can rack out after you're patched up and drop off Duke. Nick, Jordy, go rack out. Hunter and Paul, do the same once you're good to go. M." Doc ignored how the wolf didn't even acknowledge he was being addressed. "Get those wounds looked at and shift back. You know your mate is safe here."

None of the men replied, but just headed in different directions. Chuck stood next to Doug and the Mad Dogs' commanding officers while he watched Doc approach. He wasn't sure what he should, or even could, do to help the team. Chuck wasn't a part of the Mad Dogs pack, so he was surprised when Doc addressed him the same way he addressed Doug.

"You two," Doc directed his words toward both wolves so there was no doubt which of the four wolves he was addressing. "They will need to eat. So, go make them something."

"Yes, Sir," Doug replied and started toward the barracks. It wasn't until he realized that Chuck wasn't following him that he turned back to his former pack mate. "Chuck, let's go."

Chuck was dumbfounded when the Mad Dogs team leader and Alpha gave him an order as if he were part of his pack. It wasn't until Doug called out that Chuck realized he had yet to move. So, he jogged over to Doug and only once did he glance at the Med Center where his best friend had disappeared.

Rowan followed the majority of the team into the Med Center. Hunter and Paul, still in wolf form, lay together on the same bed in Med Bay One. The two patrol soldiers were in Med Bay Two when he passed and found the vampire along with the rest of the team were in Med Bay Three.

"Rowan," H began. "Drop that," he indicated the comm pack. "Strip down to your T-shirt and wash up to your elbows."

H had already stripped down, washed and bandaged Gabe's shoulder wound. He wasn't in a hurry, but Rowan didn't hesitate to do as he was ordered. By the time he was cleaned up, H had I.V. supplies, including a bag of blood for Duke and a bag of saline for B, lying next to both of his team mates. M had shifted back to his human form, for which Rowan was relieved, and stood naked beside the bed on which his bond mate lay. Rowan couldn't help but notice how M's wounds were already healed to the point the bullet wounds just appeared an angry red and Gabe was already gone.

"Alright, Rowan," H started and it pulled Rowan's attention back to the task at hand. "Duke and B are somehow connected. What happens to Duke seems to affect B. Based on what we witnessed on this mission, it's relative to proximity. So, we're gonna start with Duke."

Rowan followed H to Duke's bedside. He had had plenty of I.V.s in the past, so he was confused when H stood at the head of Duke's bed.

"Come here," H ordered. "The last time we tried to help him, he attacked."

Rowan knew his eyes had grown wide. He was aware of the damage a vampire could inflict when conscious, so he didn't even want to speculate on what Duke could do if he subconsciously reacted defensively.

"As a precaution, we will stand back here." H stepped to the side to make room for Rowan to join him behind Duke's head. "Move his arm up here," H instructed after he assembled the needle to the I.V. tubing and the tubing to the bag of blood. Rowan paid close attention to everything H did. Setting up the I.V. didn't seem difficult.

"Hold his wrist down." H applied a tourniquet high on Duke's bicep. He waited for Rowan to do as he was told and a vein to swell before he stuck Duke with the needle.

Duke's reaction was instantaneous which told H that whatever drug sedated the vampire was already wearing off. Duke's hands, claws extended, attempted to lash out above his chest. H was impressed that even though Rowan startled at Duke's violent reaction, the wolf maintained his grasp on Duke's wrist.

"Duke. You're safe, Duke," H quickly told the vampire. "We're at Camp Smokey and you're in the Med Center." H grabbed Duke's other wrist and didn't let go until his words seemed to register in the vampire's mind. "B is here, too. We are giving you blood to flush the sedative out. You need to relax, so we can tend to B."

It wasn't until Duke turned his head and spotted B that he seemed to relax. "Don't move your arm from above your head," H ordered his vampire teammate before he turned to Rowan. "Let go."

Rowan did and followed H to where he stood next to B's bed. M still made him nervous even though he had returned to his human form. He met M's gaze and his team mate's eyes no longer displayed their terrifying golden glow. That was enough to calm him somewhat.

"Ok, Rowan, start B's I.V.," H ordered and Rowan did just that. "Good," H complemented. "Now, let's take care of the others."

Rowan followed H to Med Bay Two where the human soldiers were resting comfortably on the beds. Treating their injuries was only slightly more advanced than the field treatment they already received in the Afghan cave. By the time he and H moved on to Med Bay One to tend to Hunter and Paul, both wolves were already gone.

"M can watch over B and Duke," H informed him. "Let's head to the barracks. I don't know about you, but I want a damn shower and some grub." H grinned.

"I'll just grab our stuff and equipment," Rowan replied.

"Don't worry about it." H started walking toward the door. "It's not going anywhere."

Rowan gave H a nod. "Okay."

Chuck caught sight of Rowan and H from the corner of his eye when they walked into the barracks. Neither of the wolves looked toward where he and Doug were cooking or a few of their team mates were already scarfing down food. Doug must have noticed when he turned to track Rowan's movement because his former pack mate shoulder bumped him and nodded toward where Rowan disappeared up the stairs.

"Go." Doug smiled understandingly.

"Thanks," Chuck mumbled.

He wiped his hands on a dish towel before he headed toward the stairs. There was no sign of either wolf when Chuck reached the second floor, but he could easily hear the sound of the communal shower coming from the end of the hall. It made total sense that both H and Rowan would want to wash off their mission before they ate. It was the same thing the others had done, after all.

Chuck paused in the hall. He was indecisive. *Should I go to Rowan while he's in the shower? Or, should I wait in his room?* Chuck asked himself, but it didn't take long before he came to his answer.

Just the thought of H being in the showers, as well, made up his mind. Thankfully, the door to the room Rowan claimed was slightly a jar.

Yes, I'll wait for him there, Chuck decided.

"See you downstairs."

H called out to him, but all Rowan could do was grunt by way of a reply. He really didn't think the Mad Dog expected a reply anyway which was a good thing because Rowan was enjoying the steaming hot water beating down on his neck and shoulders.

The hot shower was attempting to relax the after-mission stress out of him, but the swirling thoughts that invaded his mind made it impossible. He had caught sight of Chuck standing outside the Comm Center and again in the barrack's kitchen. This was the first mission he'd come home from where he couldn't seek out the comfort just being around his best friend seemed to provide.

Rowan could admit to himself it was his own fault this was the case. Still, he was angry. However, he was no longer sure if he was angry at Chuck's reaction to his desire to become part of the Mad Dogs pack or himself for loving his best friend enough not to do so.

Chuck would never be more than his best friend. The wolf wasn't even gay. Hell, Chuck didn't even know he was bi and in love with him. Rowan accepted it was just what it was and he'd rather have Chuck in his life as a best friend than not in his life at all.

Where does that leave us, though? Rowan thought. *We aren't even best friends anymore. And shouldn't a best friend accept what will make their best friend happy?*

Rowan turned off the shower and wrapped a towel around his waist. *My desire to join the Mad Dogs pack won't make either of us happy. So, what do I do? Give up my best friend who I love, but who will never return my feelings or throw away a life-long friendship for what I want, what feels right, and join the Mad Dogs in more than just name?*

Rowan didn't know what to do. His thoughts kept bouncing between the only two options he could see as an outcome where Chuck was concerned while he walked down the hall to his room. He was distracted when he opened the door to his room.

The sudden hitch of breath after he walked into his room and shut the door behind him was Rowan's only warning before the attack came. His body was slammed into the door behind him and even with the support of the door at his back, his arms flailed to catch his balance. A body pressed against him just as harshly as the lips that pressed against his mouth.

Rowan didn't react at all aside from flinging his arms out wide. Chuck received no response to the spontaneous kiss he leveled on his best friend. He should have known better than to throw himself at Rowan like this, but he thought if his best friend was willing to be with men sexually to join the military wolves then Rowan would be open to his advance.

Stupid, so stupid. I've made things worse. Much, much worse, Chuck berated himself when the only response Rowan gave him was becoming as still as a statue.

Rowan gained his balance and his wide surprised eyes focused on Chuck for only a moment before his best friend practically jumped back away from him. Rowan didn't move. His arms were plastered out to his sides against the door and surrounding wall from regaining his balance. His shock over what his best friend had just done was so complete he was frozen in place. The towel around his waist was now crumpled at his feet, but all his brain function was focused on what Chuck had just done.

Chuck was beyond embarrassed and humiliated. He never should have attacked Rowan as he had regardless of wanting to do just that for years. He should have known better. He should have sat his best friend down and explained how he'd wanted him for years. How it was only his jealousy over the other wolves having him just so he could be part of the military pack which caused his recent behavior.

"I'm sorry," Chuck mumbled after he stepped back a few more feet away from Rowan. If the wolf wasn't blocking the door, Chuck would flee. However, that wasn't an option. "You're not gay and I'm not one of the military pack you would be willing to join. I should have never done…"

Rowan's mind seemed to catch up to what the hell just happened here in his room. Chuck had kissed him. Actually, kissed him. Granted, he was too caught off guard to return the kiss, but his best friend had just attempted to ravish his mouth. His lack of response now had the wolf he'd loved for years feeling like he was only willing to be with a man in order to join the unit.

Well, it's time to set him straight, Rowan thought before he pushed away from the door.

Years of knowing Rowan, still didn't give Chuck any indication of the wolf's intentions when he moved away from the door. Rowan's expression hadn't changed and it took everything Chuck had not to look away from his best friend's face in order to take in the rest of his sculpted body. Since Rowan didn't appear angry, Chuck didn't retreat from where he stood. Instead, he started trying to explain again.

"I'm sorry, Rowan. I thought if you were willing to become a Mad Dog, you'd be willing…"

"More than willing," Rowan interrupted his best friend's babbling. "Willing and wanting."

Those were the last words Chuck heard before Rowan reached him, wrapped his strong arms around his waist, and plundered his mouth. It was his turn to be surprised. However, his stunned stupidity didn't last long when he felt himself pulled flush against Rowan's naked body and his best friend's tongue demanding entrance into his mouth.

Chuck opened to him and the first taste of the wolf he'd loved for years pulled a groan from deep in Rowan's chest. Just dueling with Chuck's tongue and drinking in his taste was blowing Rowan's mind to the point he couldn't help but consider this was a dream. He's dreamed about how Chuck would feel in his arms and how the wolf would taste for so long that the thought was no longer irrational.

However, feeling Chuck's hands on his naked skin and pulling him close enough his bare erection was pressing against the hard length between Chuck's legs told him no matter how many times he'd played this fantasy in his mind, this time it was real.

Chuck couldn't stop touching Rowan. He couldn't get enough of his taste, either. So, when Rowan pulled out of their kiss and moved away, Chuck could do nothing but whine like a wounded wolf.

"Are you sure?" Rowan managed to pant out even though the love and lust he could see in Chuck's deep green eyes said more than words ever could.

"Yes. More than sure for years, now," Chuck replied and pulled Rowan into another heated kiss.

Rowan pulled away again. "You're not gay."

"Less talking." Chuck didn't want to waste another minute talking. He leaned forward and nipped Rowan's lower lip.

Rowan exhaled a loud hiss when he felt Chuck's hand wrap around his cock. His head fell back of its own accord and he moaned when he felt Chuck's mouth sucking and biting on his neck. There was something he wanted to say. Something he thought he should ask, but the sensations from finally having Chuck's hands and mouth on him short circuited his brain.

Chuck maneuvered Rowan toward his bed without thought. It wasn't until he nudged Rowan just enough to fall back on his bed did his best friend seemed to come back to his senses. Rowan's pupils were blown wide with desire and Chuck's heart swelled at knowing he was the one to put that expression on Rowan's face. Rowan tried to pull him down when he fell, but Chuck was able to resist the tug to become horizontal on top of him.

Rowan's feet were still firmly planted on the floor and he gazed up at Chuck standing between his legs. As a wolf, he gave no thought to his nudity while Chuck was still dressed. However, that didn't mean he didn't want to see Chuck just as naked.

It was almost as if Chuck read his mind when the wolf toed out of his sneakers before crossing his arms to grasp the hem of his shirt to get rid of it. Next, came the jeans. Chuck unbuttoned, then unzipped them and finally kicked them off. Rowan had seen Chuck naked plenty of times before, but this time felt like the first time. In a way it was because now he could touch. He had every intention of touching Chuck's naked body, too.

Chuck wasn't going to last long. Just looking down at Rowan's muscular body sprawled out naked on the bed had him nearly ready to cum. He had a feeling Rowan wouldn't last long, either, if the way his cock was leaving a slick trail on his stomach was anything to go by. Chuck realized how long they lasted really didn't matter because this wouldn't be the last time they would be together. It was this thought that spurred him to crawl up Rowan's body.

Rowan practically held his breath and forced himself to remain still when Chuck's body slid along his. He could no longer resist moving when Chuck's lips touched his. Rowan's hands grasped Chuck's hips and pulled him down at the same time he thrust up. An almost harsh groan escaped into their kiss when Rowan felt the slide of Chuck's hard cock against his.

Chuck had to pull out of their kiss by the third time Rowan pushed up into him. The friction Rowan's cock caused against his was perfect. They were both leaking enough to provide just enough lube.

Chuck buried his head in Rowan's neck. "Fuck," he panted out. "So good."

Chuck's harsh breathing against the side of his neck and his best friend's words sent Rowan into a mind-blowing orgasm. He held Chuck's hips down so hard and flush against him he was sure his release had nowhere to go. Not that he had the brain cells to care.

Chuck felt Rowan stiffen seconds before wet warmth cocooned his cock. That was all it took. End of story. Chuck couldn't not follow Rowan into bliss.

Neither man knew or cared how long Chuck lay atop Rowan while they rode out their orgasmic high and fought to catch their breath. Neither wolf wanted to move. So, they didn't.

Chapter Fifteen

Three week later…

Oh, with El standing to the side behind him, sat at his desk and stared at his former pack mates who were seated across from him. He wasn't happy about what orders he was about to issue. However, there was nothing he could do about it. Still, he needed Doc's report first.

They all understood the pack was going to be split into two units. It was the only thing they could do in order to fight a war on two fronts. Still, Oh had hoped to have all the Mad Dogs, humans or unclaimed wolves, at Camp Smokey for a while longer. The new Mad Dogs from Nick's old pack could use more training in their new specialties and the human from the Fae's patrol, not to mention their new Fae soldier, could use more time to acclimate to the Mad Dogs. Oh envied the days McCormick only had to manage the six of Oh's old pack.

"Doc," Oh began. "Tell me how you are splitting up the Dogs."

Doc glanced at M before returning his gaze to Oh. He and M had discussed how to split up the unit several times and finally came to an agreement.

"M is going to be Bravo's team leader."

"That is obvious since he is sitting right there." Oh tried to keep his tone neutral and not let his sudden aggravation because the pack needed to be split up, spark his anger.

Doc wasn't surprised he didn't feel a damn thing through the pack link he still shared with Oh and El. They had both started shielding every time they interacted with those who used to be part of their pack.

"Bravo will consist of M as team leader, B as sniper, Hunter will do Recon, Rowan on comms, Paul will be trained as their medic, and Gabe will do Demo." Doc ignored El's smirk when he mentioned Gabe. The two were peas in a pod when it came to blowing shit up.

"You didn't mention Duke," Oh pointed out.

"Duke will be on Alpha team with me."

"Explain," Oh ordered.

"Since it seems he and B are connected in some way which caused them to share the effects of trauma if they are in a certain proximity of each other, I am separating them," Doc informed.

"And they are okay with that?" Oh raised an inquiring brow.

"They will be," Doc replied with surety.

"Alpha will comprise the rest of us," Doc began. "H comms, Nick and Jordy snipers, and Duke and the Fae, Mac, will do Recon. I will train one of the two humans to be our medic and the other will be support." Doc paused to see if Oh would comment. He didn't. "I didn't want to split them up from their patrol leader unless or until they become part of the Mad Dogs' pack," Doc finished.

"What's the status on that?" Oh hoped the humans would decide to join the pack if for no other reason than it would cement their stake in the wars.

"They haven't made up their minds and we aren't pressuring them to do so," Doc informed in a tone that clearly conveyed he wasn't about to do so, either.

"Doug will still be Alpha's HQ wolf and Chuck Bravo's," Oh stated instead of asked.

"Affirmative." Doc nodded.

Oh could find no criticism in Doc's separation of the men. So, now all he had to do was decide which mission to assign to which of his new Mad Dog units. Alpha unit was numbers heavy, but three of Doc's soldiers were untested against the type of beings the Organization used. The same could be said of Bravo as far as Nick's old pack mates were concerned. At least Nick and Jordy had been at Shadows and experienced a taste of what they could be up against. It was that thought that helped Oh decide which unit he was sending where.

Oh pulled out two folders from his desk. "Doc, your team is heading to France." Oh handed him the file. "We have Intel from the Watchers that the Organization is recruiting and setting up bases." Doc accepted the folder, but didn't bother to look through the file.

"M, your taking Bravo to Washington State. The Watchers have verified at least two locations where rogue councilmembers have been frequenting. Take them out."

"The Council doesn't want them captured?" M spoke for the first time in their meeting.

"No. Kill any you find," Oh ordered.

"Roger that." M nodded.

"Do we have any reason to be concerned the rogue councilmembers are still trying to capture one of us?" Doc inquired.

"Are either of you concerned?" Oh countered even though he was already sure of what his old pack mates' answers would be.

"No, Sir," M answered for both of them and smirked when Oh frowned. They all knew their new CO hated the military formality.

"Asshole." Oh tossed M's mission folder at him. "Read your shit and get your teams outfitted. You're leaving at 0530."

Doc and M nodded before Doc asked, "Anything else?"

"You got your orders, now get the hell out," Oh growled back.

"Yes, Sir," Doc and M said in unison again before they hustled out the door. Both Mad Dogs chuckled when they heard something crash against the door they had just closed behind them.

"So, I guess we need to brief our units," M said casually as they walked toward the barracks.

"That we do," Doc replied and tried not to think about the first missions the Mad Dogs were ordered to do as separate units.

A war on two fronts. Two Mad Dog units and only one acceptable outcome. The Mad Dogs had never failed to complete a mission. We sure as hell aren't about to start now. Doc's thoughts made him smile.

About the Author

Brenda started writing several years ago. She is an ARe (Do you remember them?) and Amazon International best-selling author. Brenda resides in Tampa, FL with her husband, six cats, a dog, and a turtle named Tammy when not attending conventions or leather/kink events.

She is active in the Tampa Bay GLBT & leather / kink community. Brenda the Ms. Florida Leather n' Fetish Pride 2016, the founder of Tampa Bay's Leather Social, and the owner (since Jan. 2016) of the Florida Leather & Fetish Pride weekend event that is held every November.

There is so much more that could be said, but that would take another novel, so check her out on Facebook!

She would love to hear from you!
Visit her on the following:

Website: www.bcothernbooks.com
Facebook: Brenda Cothern Books
Facebook Fan Page:
Brenda Cothern Books, Inc.
Goodreads: Brenda Cothern
Smashwords: BCothernBooks
Google+: Brenda Cothern Books
Twitter: BCothernBooks
Authorgraph: BCothernBooks

For signed digital autograph, please send her a request through Authorgraph! A personalized autographed PDF for the book will be signed and sent to you!

If you enjoy her books, please show your support by giving it stars and/or writing a review on the various online sites such as Amazon or Goodreads.

I would like to acknowledge and thank MLR Press (www.mlrbooks.com) for compiling the below information on the various support groups. This is one way that I 'give back' and support my GLBT community.

THE TREVOR PROJECT
The Trevor Project operates the only nationwide, around-the-clock crisis and suicide prevention helpline for lesbian, gay, bisexual, transgender and questioning youth. Every day, The Trevor Project saves lives though it's free and confidential helpline, its website and its educational services. If you or a friend is feeling lost or alone, call The Trevor Helpline. If you or a friend are feeling lost, alone, confused or in crisis, please call The Trevor Helpline.

You'll be able to speak confidentially with a trained counselor 24/7.

The Trevor Helpline: 866-488-7386

On the Web : http://www.thetrevorproject.org/

THE GAY MEN'S DOMESTIC VIOLENCE PROJECT
Founded in 1994, The Gay Men's Domestic Violence Project is a grassroots, non-profit organization founded by a gay male survivor of domestic violence and developed through the strength, contributions and participation of the community. The Gay Men's Domestic Violence Project supports victims and survivors through education, advocacy and direct services.

Understanding that the serious public health issue of domestic violence is not gender specific, we serve men in relationships with men, regardless of how they identify, and stand ready to assist them in navigating through abusive relationships.

GMDVP Helpline: 800.832.1901
On the Web: http://gmdvp.org/

THE GAY & LESBIAN ALLIANCE AGAINST DEFAMATION/GLAAD EN ESPAÑOL

The Gay & Lesbian Alliance Against Defamation (GLAAD) is dedicated to promoting and ensuring fair, accurate and inclusive representation of people and events in the media as a means of eliminating homophobia and discrimination based on gender identity and sexual orientation.

On the Web: http://www.glaad.org/
GLAAD en español:
http://www.glaad.org/espanol/bienvenido.php

SERVICEMEMBERS LEGAL DEFENSE NETWORK

Service members Legal Defense Network is a nonpartisan, nonprofit, legal services, watchdog and policy organization dedicated to ending discrimination against and harassment of military personnel affected by "Don't Ask, Don't Tell" (DADT).The SLDN provides free, confidential legal services to all those impacted by DADT and related discrimination. Since 1993, it's in house legal team has responded to more than 9,000 requests for assistance. In Congress, it leads the fight to repeal DADT and replace it with a law that ensures equal treatment for every service member, regardless of sexual orientation. In the courts, it works to challenge the constitutionality of DADT.

SLDN Call: (202) 328-3244
PO Box 65301 or (202) 328-FAIR
Washington DC 20035-5301
e-mail: sldn@sldn.org
On the Web: http://sldn.org/

THE GLBT NATIONAL HELP CENTER

The GLBT National Help Center is a nonprofit, tax exempt organization that is dedicated to meeting the needs of the gay, lesbian, bisexual and transgender community and those questioning their sexual orientation and gender identity. It is an outgrowth of the Gay & Lesbian National Hotline, which began in 1996 and now is a primary program of The GLBT National Help Center. It offers several different programs including two national hotlines that help members of the GLBT community talk about the important issues that they are facing in their lives. It helps end the isolation that many people feel, by providing a safe environment on the phone or via the internet to discuss issues that people can't talk about anywhere else. The GLBT National Help Center also helps other organizations build the infrastructure they need to provide strong support to our community at the local level.

National Hotline: 1-888-THE-GLNH
(1-888- 843-4564)
National Youth Talkline
1-800-246-PRIDE (1-800-246-7743)

On the Web: http://www.glnh.org/
e-mail: info@glbtnationalhelpcenter.org

www.ingramcontent.com/pod-product-compliance
Lightning Source LLC
Chambersburg PA
CBHW072052170626
46813CB00004B/1318